THE GYPSY QUEEN

ANNE CLEELAND

ARTEMIS PRESS

Other historical adventures from Anne Cleeland:

Tainted Angel

Daughter of the God-King

The Bengal Bridegift

The Barbary Mark

The True Pretender

A Death in Sheffield

The Spanish Mask

*For Poppy's dad, who has a bit of wanderlust, himself; and for
all others like him.*

CHAPTER 1

Captain Geordie Venables was forced to acknowledge, a bit ruefully, that he was a stubborn man. Stubborn as a mule, and look where it's got him–he'd no money, no prospects, and his horse had been stolen for the third time in a fortnight.

At present, he was wrapped in his wool army cloak, sleeping on the hard ground somewhere near San Pablo, Spain, mainly because the past few years serving in the British Army had seen him used to it, but mostly because he could ill-afford to spend the money to stay at a farmhouse. *I may have to throw it in,* he admitted, *and make for home. That, or be reduced to begging in the streets.*

Home was Melrose, Scotland—a place he hadn't seen in many a day, thanks to Napoleon's war. It was also a place he was in no particular hurry to return to, truth to tell—not when he was expected to marry the neighbor's platter-faced daughter, and take-up farming, for the merciful love of Christ. The war may be over, but on some level he was grateful for an excuse to dawdle, here in

Spain; he'd discovered that he'd a bit of wanderlust, now that he's seen some of the world, and so he was loathe to go back, just yet, and sink into the sameness of the days on a farm.

And he had good reason to stay, of course—he'd clear the Colonel's good name, or know the reason why, and he must be getting close, or he wouldn't have been warned off, in the nasty way that he was.

With a renewed purpose, he shifted his weight to find a more comfortable position. *I may be over-stubborn*, he acknowledged, *but damned if I don't think there's something to all this, and hopefully I'll get to the bottom of it, before I'm reduced to begging, in truth. At least I have my horse—a magician, that mare is, and loyal to the bone, which was more than could be said for some.*

After eight long years of war, Napoleon was being held prisoner on some island, somewhere. If it had been up to Geordie, the self-styled Emperor would have been executed the moment he was captured; a man of that stripe was not going to meekly retire from the lists—not after having come so far, so fast. But Geordie hadn't been consulted, and so–at least for the time being–there was a tentative peace in Europe, and an attempt by its war-weary inhabitants to get back to their workaday lives.

Too many lives and fortunes lost, in the meantime, and some lives harder lost than others, which was why Geordie was currently sleeping on the ground with his pockets-to-let. His commanding officer, Colonel William Merryfield, had been supposedly killed in a gambling-den fight, but Geordie wasn't having it; it was all too smoky by half, what with that Romany fellow hanging about like a dark crow, and the Colonel looking like he'd a world of hurt, sitting atop his shoulders.

One thing Geordie knew for certain; the Colonel didn't battle his way across the Peninsula because he was the type of hot-head who'd get himself killed in a gambling-den, and so Geordie suspected foul play—even more so, because no one seemed to have any interest in looking into it; not the local authorities, and not even the British Army, parts of which were still stationed here to keep the post-war peace. It was all very strange, and so—because Geordie was not one to let sleeping dogs lie—he'd begun his own search for the truth. The Colonel was a good man, and deserved better than what he'd got—a hurried funeral in San Pablo, and then buried there, with little further ado.

But all Geordie's attempts to nose-out information at the gambling-den were shunted off—had even resulted in a nasty bout of fisticuffs, that left him short a tooth. *Caught by surprise*, Geordie thought grimly; *by Christ, it won't happen again.*

To preserve his remaining teeth, he'd decided to take a different approach, and was now following up on a lead he'd been given about that smoky Romany fellow—the one who'd been hanging around the Colonel, just before he died. After accepting Geordie's last silver coin, a tall, scroungy-looking fellow had informed him that there was a gypsy troop, traveling by stealth along the River Tagus, a few miles away. "They're keeping to the countryside, because they don't want to attract any attention," the man had said in a low tone. "But if you head west along the river, you should be able to pick up their trail."

Grateful for this tip, Geordie struck out toward the river so as to track the gypsies down, and hear some answers. Unfortunately, there was little doubt that the Romanies would be even less cooperative than the gambling-den's inhabitants, but he'd see what he could see—mayhap they would be ready to pull a double-cross; the Romanies were famous for betraying a trust. If only he'd some bribe-money to flash at them—although they'd probably just rob him, and give him another beating, for his troubles. *This might be my last attempt to do justice for the Colonel,* he acknowledged reluctantly; *I am mighty tired of getting myself robbed.*

It was an unfamiliar feeling; Geordie was a big man and a seasoned soldier, and therefore not afraid to throw his fists around, if circumstances warranted. But in the past fortnight, not only had he been beaten up, he'd been robbed three times; always in the dead of night, with him all unknowing, and with poor Jenny being spirited away. Not that he really blamed the thieves; Jenny was a fine mare, and because so many horses had been killed in the war, she was a rare prize. In fact, if Jenny didn't come back this time, he might be forced to steal a horse, himself.

She'll come back, he assured himself. *She always does.*

These were lawless times, in post-war Spain, and so it wasn't worth complaining to the local authorities—in fact, they may have been orchestrating the thefts; it wouldn't come as any sort of surprise. Which meant that it was just as well that he hadn't shown anyone the mortgage, because he wasn't sure, as yet, what to make of it. He'd a soldier's instinct about self-preservation, and he didn't want to wind up with the same fate as the Colonel. That, and he'd the impression that it wasn't all on the up-and-up; although why the Colonel would hand him a fake mortgage was a very good question.

He opened his eyes to take a look at the stars—fading now, as it came on to morning. Firmly, he closed them again, and reminded himself that he needed to catch a bit of sleep, if he was going to match wits with the Romanies this day. Unfortunately, there was nothing like being robbed like a green gull to make a fellow sleep with one eye open—a bit embarrassing, it was, that he could be robbed in his sleep, after all he'd lived through. On the other hand, thievery was an honorable pursuit, in these uncertain times, and he had to grudgingly admire anyone who could take his horse, with him none the wiser.

Almost on cue, he heard a familiar nicker, and couldn't suppress a broad smile. The doughty lass had done it again, and his task tomorrow would be miles easier, now that he'd be on horseback.

Once there was sufficient daylight, Geordie examined Jenny, and found that she seemed to have suffered no harm from her adventure—which came as no surprise at all; she was as hardy a horse as he'd ever seen, and something of a survivor, same as him.

She was a black mare—glossy as a raven's wing—and deceptively solid for how well she could jump a fence. It had stood her in good stead, since obviously all the thieves who'd attempted to steal her over the past two weeks hadn't realized she could jump a three-plank fence as though it were the merest trifle. She was fast, too—and strong, since he was no lightweight, yet she never seemed to fade.

Removing his leather hat, he poured what remained of his water into it, so that she could have a drink—it must be thirsty work, to be constantly escaping. It was no hardship to him; the River Tagus was up ahead, and he'd refill his flask from there.

Affectionally, he ran a hand down her foreleg. She was

a lot like him, this mare; no one was going to take her where she didn't want to go. "Let's go, lass," he murmured. "We've some Romanies to track down."

"*Gadjo.*"

Startled, Geordie drew his pistol and aimed it in the direction of the voice, shielding himself behind Jenny. Strange; usually the horse lifted her head to warn him, if they'd an intruder, but all the blame couldn't be placed on Jenny—he was a damned nodcock, not to be paying better attention. "Who goes there?"

"No harm, no harm."

Geordie drew the hammer back, and observed the young man—a stripling, and thin—who held up his hands, and stood quietly in the shelter of the trees.

"Get along wi' you," said Geordie, not unkindly. "I'd rather not have to bury you here."

"No—I have a message for you, *gadjo*. I am to say 'stand two'."

Geordie paused in surprise. It was an Army password that they'd used in the Third Division, during the war. Interestingly, it was the password they used when there was a fear of infiltration from the enemy—it was a covert warning to be alert.

"I'm listening," said Geordie, his pistol unwavering.

"I am to give you a message."

"Let's have it, then."

Carefully, the lad reached into his shirt, and pulled forth a parchment, folded multiple times.

"What's it say?" asked Geordie.

"I do not know, *gadjo*; it is in cypher."

Debating, Geordie motioned for the lad to come

forward with the paper. "You try to take my horse, laddie, and mine will be the last face you see."

For an instant, an amused expression crossed the young man's face. "You guard that which is not yours, *gadjo*." Slowly, he offered up the note over the mare's saddle.

Geordie carefully hid his surprise, as this was, in fact, technically true. His own horse had been shot out from beneath him at the Battle of Badajoz, and Jenny had been running loose on the battlefield, having lost her own rider. As was often the case in such a situation, he'd seized her, and they'd carried on.

"Who sent you?" It seemed obvious it was someone from the Army, what with the password, and the reference to how he'd got Jenny.

"An English soldier. He says he is a friend." Pausing, the boy added, "He has sent two coins."

Geordie raised his brows, as this was of interest. It seemed unlikely the boy meant harm, if he was handing over money, but on the other hand, the code words included a warning to be wary. "Let's see them."

Again, the boy dug in his shirt and produced two silver coins, which he laid atop the saddle.

"Aye then," said Geordie, scooping them up. "Sit over there, don't move, and keep your hands where I can see them. I'm inclined to shoot, and ask questions later."

Squinting, Geordie unfolded the note, and read the contents. It was indeed in a cypher—one they'd used in the Army—and it was from Angus McDowell, a fellow Scotsman and comrade-in-arms. The message was necessarily undetailed, as was the usual case when they used a cypher, but it basically informed Geordie that Angus needed help, and that he was to follow the messenger.

Debating, Geordie eyed his companion, who was sitting cross-legged, watching Jenny crop at the grass around her feet. If Angus wanted to warn him of an ambush, he'd have planted a warning within the message, or used a different password. As it was, it seemed that he did indeed need help, but wanted Geordie to be wary, for some reason. Perhaps Angus needed reinforcements, to help him fight out of whatever trouble he was in, and the lad, here, was in for a bit of knocking-about. Geordie was not one to turn down a good set-to, so as to help out a friend, and the fact that a bit of silver had been offered made the proposition very tempting.

He addressed the boy. "Where would you take me?"

"A farmhouse, an hour's walk from here. The other English is hiding in the barn."

"He's not English, nor am I," Geordie corrected, as he rolled up his cloak. "Let's go, then."

It seemed a strange development, but Geordie was willing to take a small detour—especially if there was a payment to be had. And mayhap he'd have a chance to eat something beside the windfall apples he'd managed to gather-up yesterday—he was mighty sharp-set, and any sort of meal would be much appreciated.

Keeping a wary eye on his surroundings, Geordie followed his guide as they began to walk across the fields, leading Jenny behind them. The boy seemed uninterested in conversation, but Geordie decided he'd best reconnoiter his ground, so to speak, and so he asked in a friendly fashion, "Are you from hereabouts?"

"No, *gadjo*."

Easily, Geordie asked, "Shall I keep guessing?"

His companion glanced at him. "I am Romany. My tribe comes from the west—the Portuguese border."

Geordie nodded, and hid his surprise. Was it too much of a coincidence, that he was quietly tracking the Romanies, and then a Romany lad had been sent to divert him? It was hard to know what to think, since there was no denying that the cipher and the password were genuine. If it was only a coincidence, then this lad might know something about the Romany man who'd been hanging around the Colonel, which would be a stroke of luck; he'd try to feel him out, and see what there was to see. It might be too much to hope for, though, because there was no denying that Geordie's luck had not been very good, lately.

With a show of goodwill, Geordie offered, "We'd some help from the Romanies, during the war; they'd gather-up useful information, and pass it along."

Quickly, the boy looked up. "My father," he said. "My father would watch, and then report the number of French soldiers to the English."

"Good man," said Geordie in an approving manner, but he was to glean no further information, and it seemed that the boy regretted having said even this much. Geordie was content to walk in silence, though—all in all, the situation seemed less troublesome, if the lad's father had been willing to help the British during the war. Although—knowing what he knew of Romanies—it was just as likely that the lad's father was the one who'd been hanging around the Colonel, causing mischief. Best not to get lulled into thinking that his companion meant him well—although Geordie's initial inclination was to trust the boy. He'd commanded many a young man during the war, and he could usually make a quick and accurate assessment, being as he needed to know who was likely to stand bluff, and who was likely to falter at the first volley. This lad—this lad seemed steady, and older than his years. He'd have made a good scout, during the war— he'd that look about him.

It started to rain, but this was not a hardship, as Geordie's hat was already wet, and it meant there were fewer people about to observe them, as they circled around behind an isolated farmhouse, and then stopped a short distance away from the barn's entrance.

Wary, Geordie kept a hand on his pistol butt as the boy paused to whistle softly, the sound similar to a bird's. A few moments later, an answering bird call was heard, and the boy started forward again.

"Hold," said Geordie easily, as he snaked an arm around his companion, pinning his arms to his sides, and holding the pistol to his throat. "Now; let's go in, nice and easy, laddie."

CHAPTER 3

The Romany boy offered no resistance, and—
with a not-so-gentle nudge, just to let him
know that he meant business—Geordie prodded him
toward the barn door, which slid open a crack to reveal a
man's face, peering out at them with an impassive
expression.

"Guid mornin' to ye," said Geordie, in a broad accent.

"Let him go," the man replied. "We mean no harm."

"I'll hear from Angus, first."

The man considered this, and then he nodded,
opening the door wide, and gesturing them within.
Carefully keeping his distance, Geordie sized-up the
fellow, and decided he might be a Romany, too—although
his skin was a lighter shade than the lad's. He was just
under six feet, and looked as though he knew how to
handle himself, which was something to think about, if
the situation were to devolve into a set-to—Geordie
didn't much like the odds.

"My horse comes in," Geordie said. "I can't leave her without, to catch someone's fancy."

"Yes; I understand," the other agreed, and then he turned to walk into the barn's interior. Warily, Geordie followed, holding the lad in a firm grip as Jenny's hooves clip-clopped on the wooden plank floor.

Their guide paused outside an empty stall and gestured to Geordie. "Here."

Almost immediately, Geordie heard a familiar voice. "Cap'n? Is that you?"

With no small relief, Geordie loosed the boy, and strode over to the stall's entry to take-in the sight of Angus, propped up in a corner amongst the straw and wrapped in a blanket—although the morning was not cold, only wet. Sitting next to him was a young woman— a peasant woman, mayhap; she wore a full skirt and had a figured scarf, twisted around her head. Her arms were clasped around her knees as her gaze rested upon Geordie and the boy for a moment, and then she ducked her head.

With an effort, Angus hoisted himself to his feet, and Geordie quickly stepped forward to assist him, having glimpsed the patch of dried blood on the man's shirt, where the blanket had fallen away. "Lord alive; you're wounded, man. What's happened?"

Gingerly, the older Scotsman flexed a shoulder. "I'll have it seen to, Cap'n—but I'll be needin' a favor, if ye dinna mind."

"Name it."

"The girl—" here, the man indicated the seated figure with a nod of his head. "I was hired as a mercenary, for protection. I was to deliver her to her bridegroom, in exchange for a round payment, but instead I was ambushed on the road."

Geordie drew his brows together—no question there were roving bands of outlaws scattered throughout Spain, many of them ex-soldiers who were taking advantage of the current lawlessness. "Who were they—did you see?"

Angus shrugged. "Dunno. Four o' 'em–Romanies from another tribe, these ones say. They wanted 'er." Again, he used his head as an indicator. "I gave 'em a few blasts, and they scattered, but I got meself winged, in the retreat." He then jerked his chin toward the boy. "I knew you was summat about here, and so I sent the laddie out to find ye—look for a bonny black mare, I tole him."

Nodding thoughtfully, Geordie glanced at the girl again. "And who is she, that she's such a prize?"

"She's gypsy royalty—their Queen, or some sech, and everyone's fightin' over what's to become of her, on account of the war's havin' killed so many of them off. The other tribes are wantin' to seize her for themselves, and that's why these ones hired an escort, so as to deliver her to her weddin'."

Geordie kept his expression unreadable, but he was somewhat relieved, all in all. This tale verified the tale he'd been told by the fellow at the gambling-den—that a Romany tribe was traveling along the river, but trying to keep their presence quiet. If the object was to form an alliance against the other tribes who were also struggling to survive, it all made sense—in fact, it was very similar to what was happening on a larger scale, with all the countries in Europe trying to negotiate their own new alliances, after the war.

Yet again, however, it seemed almost an impossible stroke of luck—that Geordie had been asking some questions about that Romany fellow who'd been hanging around the Colonel, that he'd been promptly beaten-up for his pains, and now a Romany tribe was enlisting him to help them. After all, it didn't take a genius to see the "favor" that Angus wanted from him. *Be wary, laddie;* he warned himself. *There's a few too many coincidences, here.*

With a smile, Geordie chided, "For the holy love of Christ, Angus—how did the likes of you get enlisted to deliver-up a Gypsy Queen?"

His answering smile a bit sheepish, the older man shrugged. "They wanted a British soldier, so's that everyone would think twice afore comin' at her—no one wants to cross the British, nowadays."

"That plan didn't much work," Geordie observed.

"I know, I know—caught me by surprise, the thievin' bastards." Angus paused, and glanced up at Geordie from beneath his bushy brows. "But they're willin' to pay ten gold pieces."

As this was indeed a princely sum, Geordie whistled softly. "As much as that? I didn't know there was anyone left in Spain, with that kind o' money."

Angus nodded, and cut to the nub. "I'll halve it with ye, if ye can deliver her."

Geordie tilted his head, pretending to consider the offer. "Where's she to be delivered?"

"This lot is to meet-up with the other tribe about seven

miles down the river—you could do it in a day. A fine payment, for a day's work."

Geordie decided he may as well point out the obvious. "And what makes you think these Romanies are going to follow through with the promised payment, Angus? The ambush may have been their work, instead."

But the other Scotsman shook his head. "No point in ambushin' me—my pockets are to let. And you can see that it's important to them—like I said, she's some sort o' royalty, and they need to make this alliance with the other tribe, as quick as can be."

Geordie nodded—he'd fall in with the scheme, of course. This set-up was as smoky as all get-out, and he didn't trust any of them—even Angus—worth a tinker's damn, but he'd already got two silver coins out of the deal, and it seemed clear that he was being drawn-in, for some reason. With any luck, he'd come out of this bramble-bush five gold coins the richer, in addition to gleaning whatever information he could about the Colonel's death. And even if he didn't glean much, with that kind of money he'd be able to toss out a few bribes, here and there, which should help loosen some lips.

He took another assessing look at the lass, and caught her covertly studying him, beneath her lashes. Her eyes were a clear, pale green and rather startling, against her dark eyelashes, and tanned face. When she dropped her gaze, he asked Angus a bit brusquely, "Was she injured, too?"

"No—they don't dare hurt her, she's the prize."

Geordie agreed, "I'll do it, then—and you'd best see a medico."

"Aye, Cap'n; there's an old medico upriver—an infantryman, and used to stitchin' up holes."

Geordie nodded. "Good. I'll come seek you out then, once I've been paid." He glanced down at the lass again. "How do you communicate—does she speak Spanish?"

Angus raised his brows. "She speaks English, Cap'n."

Startled, Geordie met the girl's eyes and saw that she smiled slightly, in wry acknowledgment; he should not have spoken so freely, but it was too late, now.

Angus gathered-up his blanket, and nodded in gruff gratitude. "Thank ye, Cap'n; I'd have been that sorry to miss the payout—it's sore needed, nowadays."

Geordie tilted his head. "Dinna fash yourself, man; see to your hurts, and I'll meet up with you as soon as may be." Affably, he reached to shake the other's hand. "Stand two?"

"Stand two," the other man agreed. He then trudged out the barn door, pulling his battered hat low over his face against the rain, which was now gusting outside.

Into the silence, Geordie sighed heavily. "Aye, then; someone's going to tell me what in Christ's name is going on, here."

CHAPTER 4

There was a small silence, and no one moved. The man asked, "What do you mean, Captain?"

With a casual movement, Geordie threw an arm across Jenny to hide the fact he was surreptitiously reaching for his pistol. "Angus kept forgetting which shoulder was wounded." With a lowered brow, he fixed his gaze on the boy. "And you didn't trace me by my bonny black mare, laddie, because my bonny black mare was stolen two days ago, and only found her way back to me early this morn."

Carefully, he watched their reactions, and noted that the girl lowered her gaze to the straw, whilst the boy's eyes slid to the man, briefly.

"Who are you?" Geordie addressed the other man bluntly. "And why the charade?"

There was a small silence, and then the man slowly replied, "What your friend told you is true. We seek to deliver the Queen to the bridegroom, so as to create a stronger alliance."

Geordie nodded, as this rang true. "Fair enough. Why did you want to switch-out Angus for me?"

"Your friend believed that you would be better-suited for the task. He also believed that if you thought him injured, you'd be more likely to offer your help."

This, in fact, was plausible—and it would explain Angus' play-acting; he may have thought the job was beyond his own powers, but was too ashamed to simply claim a one-half finder's fee outright, and so he sought to justify it by feigning an injury. This would also explain something that had puzzled Geordie from the first; he knew how men behaved, just after they'd been in a fight for their lives, and he didn't have the sense that such a thing had actually occurred.

On the other hand, Geordie wouldn't be surprised if yet again, he wasn't hearing the full tale; Angus himself had given him a covert warning to be wary, and the lass —the lass was brimful o' secrets, as his mother used to say.

As though aware that their visitor was not yet persuaded, the man said a few words to the young woman in another language, and she nodded. With nimble fingers, she turned over the hem of her skirt to extract a gold coin, from where it was secreted within.

"A goodwill offering," said the man, as he took the coin from her palm and handed it to Geordie. "Please accept it, along with our apologies for having misled you."

"I will, then," Geordie said, as he secured the coin in

his waistcoat. "And I should point out that you seem a bit too trusting, for Romanies."

"Perhaps," the man agreed, with a faint smile. "The circumstances being what they are, we are left with little choice."

"Let's have your names, then," Geordie said. "So's I can give you your orders."

"I am Marcello," the man replied. "This is Adao, and this is Queen Etta."

Geordie nodded to the others before he crouched down, and brushed aside some straw from the wooden floor. "Make a map, then, to show me where it is we're going."

Marcello crouched beside him, and made a crude rendering of the river. "We are here. There is a bend in the river, about seven miles south, and that is our destination. There are no settlements to speak of, along the route, which is why it was chosen; we seek to avoid scrutiny. We are to meet the bridegroom's representatives here, at their camp." He drew a mark with his finger, inland from the river bend. "There is a village nearby—Santa Luisa."

Geordie nodded, and bent his head to study the map. He had the niggling feeling that Marcello wasn't yet telling him the truth, but Geordie was inclined to accept the tale at face value—if their object had been to do him harm, they'd have already made the attempt, here at this isolated farmhouse. On the other hand, it was well-known that the Romanies were a secretive bunch, and so the man may be reluctant to tell a stranger much of anything, other than the bare minimum necessary to complete the assignment—if the assignment was what they'd said it was. Again, it seemed far too coincidental that he'd managed to fall into this happenstance, just after he'd been given a bit of beat-up for making inquiries about a Romany man. He'd be careful, and see what there was to see. It did seem that they'd the gold to give him, as promised, so that even if they double-crossed him, his pockets would be the richer for it, compared to how they were this morning.

Rising to his feet, Geordie said, "I'll put the Queen up on Jenny, and lead her—we'll walk along the river's edge, since that takes away one angle of attack. The both of you will watch the exposed flank, and stay out of sight. Do you have weapons?"

"We do," said Marcello. After hesitating for a moment, he added, "Shouldn't the horse be hidden, Captain? She may draw unwanted attention."

"She's a trained war-horse," Geordie explained. "If we're attacked, I'll pull the Queen down, and the horse knows to act as a shield while I'm returning fire. She's done it afore, plenty of times."

"I see," Marcello said.

"Not to mention she's recognizable, as belonging to me," Geordie continued, as he lifted a stirrup, to check the cinch. "With any luck, that will make any troublemakers think twice—I'm not easily beat." He cocked his head. "But Angus was right; best to do the journey all in a day, and keep moving. I'd not want to be exposed in this area, after dark."

"Very good," Marcello agreed.

Geordie turned to Queen Etta, and held out a hand. "Up you go, then. We haven't a proper ladies' saddle, but we'll be walking, so it shouldn't be too much of a hardship."

In a businesslike manner, Geordie hoisted the young woman atop Jenny. She was a comely lass—now that he'd a good look at her—and with as pretty a set of ankles as he'd ever seen, since her skirts didn't cover her feet, once she was seated atop the horse. A comely lass, but he'd best keep a careful distance between them; Romany women had notoriously loose morals, and he didn't want her thinking he'd be willing to dally. Not that there'd be much chance for such, of course—what with her wedding in the offing, and her being royalty, and all.

Because he was nevertheless aware that he wasn't inclined to follow this sound advice, he sternly warned himself, *You're to behave yourself, laddie; keep your lusty thoughts on all that gold, instead.*

"Who's who?" Geordie asked, as he led Jenny along the pathway next to the river. The Gypsy Queen had made no attempt at conversation thus far, which was just as well, since beneath his ambling, relaxed posture, Geordie had been on high alert for the past several hundred yards; his hand resting on the pistol in his coat pocket.

Thus far, however, everything seemed peaceful. The rain had mostly cleared, but the clouds and mud meant that there'd be few others, out and about this morning, which was to the good. Cautiously, he relaxed a bit, and decided that a bit of probing would be in order—he'd get the lass to talking, and glean whatever information he may.

"Who's who, what?" she replied, and he could hear the smile in her voice.

Without looking back at her, Geordie answered, "Our friend Marcello didn't want to explain the relationship between the three of you."

"I am not surprised," she replied, and offered nothing more.

Geordie lifted his head, and thoughtfully surveyed the tree tops that lined the river. "I've never heard that language he spoke to you, and in my time, I've heard plenty."

"I do not doubt it," she agreed, in all admiration. "You seem very well-traveled."

He could not suppress a smile, and warned, "I'll find out, you know. I'm like a terrier with a bone."

"Are you? That is very reassuring."

He lifted a corner of his mouth, and tried a different tack. "A shame, that you have need of a guard in the first place. A wedding should be a happy occasion."

"That is true," she agreed.

As she made no further response, he doggedly continued, "Who is it, that's coming after you?"

Readily, she answered, "The *Cujans*. I am betrothed to the head of the *Tsiganoi* tribe, and the *Cujans* do not wish my tribe to be allied with his in such a way—they fear it would weaken their own standing."

To his ears, her answer seemed a bit too glib, as though it had been rehearsed, even though he'd no reason to doubt the tale. He knew the Romany tribes tended to quarrel—especially in this region, where the Balkan tribes rubbed up against the European tribes—and they'd have even more incentive now, with the war having made everyone's survival that much more difficult. So; it was plausible that another tribe might want to seize this Gypsy Queen for themselves—either to marry her outright, or to hold her for ransom. On the other hand, he'd the persistent sense that he was not hearing the full tale.

"Seems a bit desperate," he said aloud. "That they'd be so bold as to seize you, and provoke a quarrel."

"I bring a handsome dowry." There was a thread of amusement in her voice—she seemed mightily amused, for a bride in danger–but this was a good point, and one that he'd overlooked; these people were tossing silver and gold coins about like seed for the birds, so it did appear that they were from a wealthy tribe. In these uncertain times, a handsome dowry might be the only thing between a gypsy tribe and starvation, and so it would be a massive incentive to try to seize the girl, so as to force her into marriage. Not to mention there was the obvious draw; she was a comely lass, for a Romany. In his experience, Romany woman tended to be a bit more— more *earthy*, but this girl's hands—her hands were slim and graceful, and didn't look workworn at all.

Abruptly putting a firm stop to this train of thought, he brought his mind back to the matter at hand. "So; where's your betrothed, in all this? Why isn't he the one who's providing a guard?"

Again, she had a ready answer. "His tribe comes ten days' journey, from the Brittany coast. Santa Luisa seemed a good meeting-place, between us."

At this, he glanced back at her in surprise. "You haven't yet met the man?"

"No, Captain; I have not."

Again, he had the quick impression that she was amused by his reaction, and he shook his head as he brought his attention back to the path ahead. "Fah; that seems barbaric, to my way of thinking. In Scotland, a lass canno' be handed over in such a way, will-she or nil-she."

"Unfortunately, these are barbaric times."

This was true, of course, and none knew it better than Geordie, who'd managed to survive the bitter and hard-fought Peninsular Campaign. And—as he'd already acknowledged—the Romanies were only doing on a smaller scale the same thing that was happening amongst all the European nations; everyone was frantically working to shore up their defenses against those who sought to take advantage of the chaotic situation. A shame, that this bonny lass was to be sacrificed for the greater good, but—as the lass herself had said—these were hard times. Not that she seemed very unhappy about it—she seemed almost cheerful, in fact, beneath her calm manner. No doubt she'd been raised to understand her role.

The girl's voice interrupted his thoughts. "Why are *you* here, Captain?"

Geordie decided that he could give as good as he got, in the secrets-keeping, and answered easily, "Ach, I'm here for the fishing."

"Ah," she said, and he heard the smile in her voice, again. "What is it you hope to catch? Bluegill?"

Surprised, he slowed so that he came even with Jenny's head, and glanced up at the lass. "And what is 'bluegill'?"

"A freshwater fish." She held up her hands to show him. "This size. White flesh, with many bones."

"Trout, mayhap," he guessed. "We call it trout, where

I'm from. And damned if I don't wish I had one right now —the very thought of it is making my mouth water."

"I have a drop-line," she offered.

He stared into her clear green eyes, alight with amusement, and found he was having trouble finding his voice. "You have a drop-line?" *Laddie*, the voice in his head warned; *watch yourself.*

She nodded. "Yes. It is in my tote-bag."

He dug into his coat pocket, and unwrapped a kerchief to expose his own drop-line—a small, wooden frame, with fishing twine wrapped tightly around it.

"Oh—may I see?" She held out her hand, her interest keen.

Laddie, he warned himself; *laddie, don't be a fool.* "Mind the hook," he told her, and handed it over.

"It is quite old," she observed, her brow knit, as she examined the weathered prongs with deft fingers.

"It was my father's, afore me." *Laddie, Laddie—*

She glanced up to meet his gaze. "What else do you carry, there in your kerchief?"

He saw that she referred to how he'd tied-up a corner of the small square of cloth, and with a show of solemnity, he looped Jenny's rein over his arm, and carefully untied the knot to reveal what was contained within.

"Oh," she faltered. "I—I see."

"My poor tooth," he announced. "Lost it in a fight, three days since."

"That is indeed a shame," she offered, her smooth brow knit with concern. "Does it hurt?"

In a grave tone, he teased, "No, lass. I'm hoping to find an apothecary, to have him pop it right back in." This was nonsense, of course—once a tooth was out, it was out, but he didn't want to tell her that the true reason he kept the tooth was to ram it down the throat of the fellow who'd knocked it out. Say what you will, the Scots knew a thing or two about vengeance.

"Oh," she said, trying to hide her dismay at this rather naive plan. Diplomatically, she offered, "I hope it works out as you wish."

Unlikely, he thought, as he grimly turned back to resume his journey. *Because now I'm saddled with yet another burdensome task; not only do I have to find out what happened to the Colonel, I've got to find some way to marry this Gypsy Queen for myself.*

CHAPTER 6

*H*ard on this unexpected epiphany, the girl's voice floated out from behind him. "Tell me; what sort of fish do you catch in Scotland, Captain?"

Instantly, Geordie was on high alert. *You may be fair besotted, laddie,* he acknowledged, *but it's clear she's trying to take your attention away from something—she's not one to natter.*

"Salmon, mostly," he answered in an offhand tone, his keen glance resting on the two fisherman who were seated in a wooden dory, just off shore. "Would that I had some right now; I am mighty sharp-set."

"I am not familiar with 'salmon'," she offered in a cheerful tone. "How is it best prepared?"

"Baked on the coals, outdoors," he replied absently. "Hold a moment, and let me see if these two have any fish to spare."

He dropped Jenny's reins, and with a purposeful stride, approached the river's edge so as to signal to the two men. It was a bit strange, now that he thought about it; neither one of them had so much as lifted his head, to take a gander at a pretty girl on a fine black mare, passing so close by. "Ho, there," he called to them. "Have you any fish to sell?"

Startled, the taller of the two glanced up at him from under the broad brim of his leather hat, and then quickly lowered his face to shake his head. "No, *señor*. No fish."

"A shame," said Geordie, eyeing the shorter man, who hadn't looked up at all. "Although the worst day fishing is better than the best day farming."

"*Si*," the taller man agreed briefly, and then looked up in astonishment, as Geordie suddenly plunged into the river, wading so as to quickly catch hold of the dory's side.

"*Gadjo!*" he called out in alarm. "What—"

But Geordie had already lunged to grasp hold of his collar, and then haul him over the side with great force, so that his head was submerged in the river as he struggled frantically against Geordie's iron grip.

After what he deemed was an appropriate length of time, Geordie pulled the gasping man's head out of the river. "Talk," he commanded. A bit grimly, he noted that neither Marcello nor Adao had come forward to offer their aid, and that the lass had made no sound of alarm, behind him.

"*Señor—señor*; please, I—I don't understand," the taller man sputtered, and Geordie immediately shoved his head back into the water again.

The shorter man watched his companion's struggles with a pained expression. "Please—there is no call for such measures, *Ingles*."

"Not *Ingles; Escocés.*"

The shorter man did not appear to understand the distinction, and so he diplomatically amended, "No need for trouble, *señor.*"

Geordie pulled his victim up, and allowed him to gasp for a moment. "You will tell me what is afoot here, or I will drown you, here and now." He'd recognized the taller fellow as his informant from the gambling-den— the one who'd given him the information about the Romany tribe's whereabouts—and this was one coincidence too many. There was obviously some plan afoot; it might be an ambush, but damned if there would be any point in ambushing Geordie, and certainly no point in coming up with the elaborate Gypsy Queen story, if a simple robbery was the object. Something else was at play, and he'd best find out what it was, and as soon as may be. In the process, he should try not to injure any of them overmuch, being as he was going to wind up with the girl, and he didn't want to start off on the wrong foot.

"Captain—" Etta called out tentatively.

"In a minute, lass," he called back, and roughly shook the gasping man, "Ready to talk? Why did you prod me to come here, and meet-up with these others?"

Whilst the wetted man struggled with how best to answer, Geordie was unsurprised to hear Marcello's voice, behind him. "They are with us, Captain."

"Then we'll need to have a bit of a discussion," Geordie said in a sour tone, and shoved the man back against the boat with a great deal of force. "I don't much like being lied to."

"My apologies, again," said Marcello. "No harm was intended."

"I'll be the judge o' that." Grimly, Geordie glanced overhead. "It's looking to rain again, so we may as well find another barn to duck into, and parley."

"Very well," Marcello agreed. There is a homestead up the river—a mile, perhaps."

"Good," said Geordie. "You go ahead, and we'll meet you there. Send the boy to direct me when you've reconnoitered."

"You will be left unguarded," Marcello cautioned.

"He'll come with me," Geordie said, referring to the shorter man in the boat. "And my wet friend, here, will take your place on the flank, and stay out-of-sight in the trees."

This strategy agreed upon, the party broke up, and Geordie took up Jenny's reins again, wishing his boots weren't thoroughly wet, and hoping the others would have the sense to start a fire as soon as they'd found a place to shelter.

They walked for a few paces in silence, whilst Geordie's new companion hurried to keep up with Geordie's longer strides. He was an older man, with uneven tufts of grizzled hair that poked out below a pointed hat, giving him a rather clownish appearance. He didn't seem very bright—or brave, for that matter— which was to the good; Geordie had developed a keen sense as to who could stand in the gap and who was a weak link, so to speak, and he very much suspected that this little fellow could be persuaded to give up some information.

"You a Romany?" Geordie began.

"*Si*. I am Minos." The shorter man looked up at Geordie, and offered a nervous, conciliatory smile.

"Who's the other man?"

"Gaston," Minos replied. "He is a *Rom*, too."

"But not Spanish."

"No—Gaston is from a different tribe. He means no harm, *gadjo*."

"I'll be the judge o' that," Geordie reiterated, and then lowered his voice, so that the girl on the horse behind them could not overhear. "Tell me this, Minos; are either one of you kinfolk to Queen Etta?"

The man looked at him, baffled. "Kinfolk?"

"Aye–kinfolk. Family." Lord alive, no one around here could speak simple English.

Minos shook his head, as he hurried alongside Geordie. "Oh no, *gadjo*. She is the *Rom Chey* of her tribe."

"Which means?"

The man considered. "Her father was the *Rom Baro*, but now he is dead, and therefore she is the *Rom Chey* —she is the daughter, who must be married to preserve his honors. Their tribe is very wealthy, and has many horses."

"And where do they come from?" Etta seemed vaguely Italian, to him, despite the fact that Adao had said they were from the Portuguese border. After eight years of war, a fellow got good at discerning who was from where, as a survival mechanism.

Mino's expression grew pensive. "Her tribe–the *Calé*–

traveled around Portugal and southern Spain, but they suffered many losses, after the Battle of Évora. Now they are scattered, and few remain."

Geordie nodded, as this fit in with what Adao had told him; Geordie's sense that the lass wasn't Portuguese must be wrong, then. "And now the tribes are fighting over who she's to marry? The man who marries her will be the next *Rom Baro?*"

The Romany man looked over at Geordie in surprise. "Who is fighting over her, *gadjo?*"

Geordie was surprised in his own turn. "Isn't there a rival Romany tribe, looking to seize her?"

Minos cocked his head, openly skeptical. "This is unlikely; no one would dare cross the Frenchman."

Oh-ho, Geordie thought; *now we're getting somewhere.* "And who is the Frenchman?"

The man made a derisive sound, and then leaned to spit on the ground. "Rochon, Napoleon's man. He moves the chess pieces, still."

Geordie considered this in silence, a bit taken aback. Since Napoleon had been soundly defeated, it seemed very unlikely that any of his people would still hold sway, here in Spain. This Romany man appeared to be sincere, though—although he was a Romany, and so all shows of sincerity should probably be taken with a pinch of salt. Not to mention that he and Marcello didn't appear to have consulted with each other over their story, which seemed a little strange—although it was likely that Minos was speaking out of turn, and that Marcello wouldn't be best-pleased to hear of it.

Geordie walked for a few paces, watching ahead for

Adao, and thinking over this unexpected and rather unsettling news. If it was true that the Romanies had dealings with Napoleon's people, that would make the Colonel's death—and Geordie's own misfortunes—all the more ominous. Not to mention it would mightily complicate his plan to steal the gypsy bride, if he was to have to contend with enemy forces.

Aloud, he said, "That's a bit hard to believe, friend; why would Napoleon's man meddle in a Romany marriage?"

His companion shrugged. "I know not. I only know that Rochon insists on the marriage, and so married they will be—no one dares to cross Rochon."

"Who is the bridegroom?" Geordie asked, glancing down at him. "Do you know him?"

The smaller man shrugged. "A *Rom* who is valuable to Rochon."

"Why? Why is he valuable?"

"I do not know, *gadjo*." Minos replied, panting slightly with the exertion of keeping up. "We do not ask questions. We have little choice, but to do as Rochon directs."

"And why is that?" Geordie persisted. "It makes no sense; if this Rochon fellow was Napoleon's man, during the war, he has no power over anyone, anymore—he should be grateful he's not in prison."

"No one dares to cross Rochon," his companion repeated. "He is a very dangerous man."

We'll just have to see about that, thought Geordie, and then pulled down the brim of his hat, in a gesture many a soldier had seen, just before charging into battle.

CHAPTER 7

*I*n due course, Adao appeared to direct them to a farmhouse, where the others had arranged for the use of the barn and—thank the Lord—had a fire already burning in a brazier. The rain had begun in earnest, and so—all in all—it was just as well that they'd had to take this little detour. With any luck, Geordie would be able to further unravel this strange situation, because there were several points that didn't make much sense to him. Despite the briar-patch of lies he was having to hack through, he didn't have the feeling that he was in any danger—he'd developed a well-honed sense for it, over the past few years. Nonetheless, it would pay to be wary; after all, Angus had given him a warning, and the next thing he knew, a band of gypsies was seeking his supposed help, even though their tale kept unpeeling like an onion.

As he pulled off his boots, and set them to dry by the brazier, Geordie asked Marcello, "What did you tell the homesteaders?"

"I told the man and his wife that we were traveling to a wedding, and we didn't wish to be caught in the rain. I paid them, and so they were happy to offer their barn, and a kettle of soup."

This was welcome news, since Geordie was as empty as a pocket, and was half-inclined to start chewing on his soggy boot. "We'll talk whilst we eat, then."

Adao spoke up. "I have asked for vinegar and mustard, *gadjo*; I would like to apply a poultice to the mare's knees."

"I've no objection; thank you, lad." This was an unlooked-for boon; Jenny could use such a treatment, in this weather, and after jumping over an unknown number of fences when she'd escaped from wherever she'd been, the night before. The Romanies were famously good with horses, so he'd no fears the boy would botch it.

The homesteaders brought out the steaming kettle, along with a loaf of day-old bread, and the men took up their wooden bowls and settled around the brazier to eat. Adao and the lass—Queen Etta, supposedly—sat at a small distance on milking stools, with Etta offering her assistance as the lad wrung-out strips of linen soaked in hot water, and bound them to Jenny's knees.

Watching the girl's graceful movements, Geordie was subject to a powerful tug of attraction that was hard to ignore, now that she'd removed her colorful headscarf so that it could dry by the brazier. Her hair was bound back, long and dark and stick-straight— not even a stray curl, as a result of the rain; hair like the girls from China, but she wasn't from China—although she had those high cheekbones. That straight hair definitely didn't look Italian, but it didn't look Portuguese, either. Was she Greek, mayhap? It hardly mattered; she was slender and winsome and she was paying absolutely no attention to him, which was a shame, being as they were going to spend the rest of their lives together.

"What is it you wish to know, Captain?"

With a mental sigh, Geordie pulled his attention back to Marcello, who, he suspected, was none too pleased that the *gadjo* was caught-out eyeing the Gypsy Queen. "It seems clear that I'm being steered, and I'd like to know why—to what purpose?"

Marcello had a ready answer. "Your friend felt you would be more suited to the task ahead than he."

"No need to monitor me, then. Who are the other two reporting to?" With a casual gesture, Geordie ate a spoonful of soup, and waited.

Marcello ducked his head, considering his answer. "Minos and Gaston are from the bridegroom's tribe."

Geordie refrained from pointing out that this did not jibe with what Minos had told him, and only nodded. Of the two versions, he was inclined to believe Minos', since Etta had said the bridegroom's people were from Brittany, and Gaston seemed vaguely French to him. Minos, on the other hand, seemed Spanish, but he'd a Greek name, so it was anybody's guess where he was from. It was possible that a single Romany tribe might include more than one nationality, but Geordie very much doubted it; the tribes kept to themselves, and tended to be nomads. Only one thing seemed clear—Marcello was shading the truth, yet again. It was a bit surprising to Geordie, all in all;

Marcello appeared to be an upright sort of fellow, who chose his words carefully—he clearly seemed the leader, in this group. But it did not bode well, that the man felt it necessary to continually mislead him; Angus was right—there was more afoot here than it seemed.

Keeping these rather troubling thoughts to himself, Geordie asked Marcello, "If they're from the bridegroom's tribe, why would they be spying on me?"

"It was the bridegroom's wish."

Geordie paused in eating, and did not hide his surprise. "The *bridegroom* wanted me to be monitored?"

The other man nodded. "Yes. It is at the bridegroom's request that you are here at all."

His brow knit in bewilderment, Geordie stared at him. "Why does the bridegroom want me involved?"

"He said he knows you—he knows you from your time in the British Army, and believes that you would be helpful, in this situation."

Carefully keeping his puzzled frown in place, Geordie bent over the soup again, so as to hide his extreme satisfaction. "I wasn't acquainted with any Romanies in the Army, friend."

But this was not exactly true; he'd known of one Romany in particular—the scroungy little fellow who was thick-as-thieves with Colonel Merryfield, just before the Colonel had been killed. Lord alive, what a stroke of luck; the bridegroom must have information for Geordie— information about the Colonel's death. It was the only logical explanation, and it all fit; this Romany bridegroom had heard that Geordie was asking questions about the Colonel, and now he'd found a way to pass information on to him, all quiet-like, with no one the wiser. Small blame to the man for being so wary; after all, whoever was behind the Colonel's death hadn't hesitated to rough-up Geordie, and that was no easy task.

He paused for a moment, thinking this over. This theory didn't seem to make a lot of sense, though; why not send a note, through Angus? They'd already made use of the cypher, why not pass along whatever information the bridegroom wanted to tell him in that way? It seemed as though this bridegroom-fellow needed Geordie to be standing before him, for some reason. Mayhap he needed to make certain Geordie was on the up-and-up, before he said anything? But that didn't make much sense either, since Angus would have vouched for him.

The only explanation that he could think of, was that the bridegroom needed to speak to him in person— mayhap he wanted to probe Geordie for information, in turn, and he didn't want the others to hear it.

It truly didn't matter—if this *Rom Baro* bridegroom needed information, Geordie would be glad to give it to him, in exchange for whatever the man could pass along about the Colonel's death. Geordie would then thank him kindly, steal his bride away, and call it a good day's work.

These promising thoughts were interrupted when Adao came over to settle on the floor beside him, and look into the contents in Geordie's bowl. "Are you going to eat that, *gadjo?*"

Geordie relinquished the remainder with good grace, even though he hadn't eaten his fill—he remembered what it was like to be a stripling, and constantly starving.

As Adao wolfed down the soup, Marcello spoke into the silence. "And now I must confess that your task involves more than we've led you to believe."

Geordie cocked his head, unsurprised. "Aye, then. Let's hear it."

"The bridegroom is being held prisoner in the Alcazar."

Geordie turned to stare at him in the silence that this revelation deserved. "The *Alcazar*?" Lord alive, this tale grew stranger and stranger; the Alcazar was a Spanish presidio—just outside of Santa Luisa, if memory served. "I don't understand; you want me to break a prisoner out of the Alcazar? Are you daft, man?"

"No—no; the authorities have agreed to allow us in for the wedding." Marcello paused, and then offered rather obliquely, "I will also tell you that you were recruited, because it is hoped that you will scout the facility for weaknesses, while we are inside."

Geordie drew his brows down. "You *are* daft, if you think a band of gypsies can take-down the Alcazar. Not to mention that I'll not be a party to starting-up another war."

"I'm afraid another war is inevitable, Captain," Marcello replied in a grave tone. "Within the next year, perhaps."

Geordie considered this unwelcome disclosure with a scowl, and ran an irritated hand over his face. The Romanies were usually right with their information, which is why the British had been so eager to recruit them, during the past war. "Is that so? What have you heard?"

Rather than answer, Marcello said, "To this end, it is important that the Alcazar be scouted for weaknesses."

"Is there a Frenchman, within?" Geordie guessed, remembering what Minos had told him.

But Marcello only replied in a steady tone, "You must not speak of the Frenchman, Captain. Nor of anything else we tell you."

In the ensuing silence, Geordie rested his hands on his knees and digested this information; it seemed this tale had more twists and turns than a rabbit warren, but he was starting to see a glimmer of logic, in how it was unfolding. Apparently, the Alcazar was some sort of headquarters for the remnants of Napoleon's army, working secretly to start-up another war. And it also seemed likely that the British Army had caught wind of this fact, and had asked these gypsies to reconnoiter the interior, under the guise of delivering a gypsy bride to her bridegroom.

He could see the wisdom in such a plan; the British were supposed to be engaged in peace negotiations in Vienna, but if the enemy was using the Alcazar to plot out mischief, they could enlist these gypsies to have a look 'round, with no one the wiser.

However, there were several points that still didn't make much sense; if it was truly the British Army who was trying to infiltrate the Alcazar, why wouldn't they just approach Geordie, and ask him outright for his help? Why all this roundaboutation, with Angus' tale of injury-by-ambush, and gypsy spies, posted along the route?

And—come to think of it—if the British Army was sending him on an unsanctioned spying mission, then

Geordie's earlier theory—that the bridegroom must know something about Colonel Merryfield's death—was wrong, and there would be no information passed along. But *surely*, it couldn't be a coincidence—that he'd been roughed-up for asking questions about a Romany man, and the next thing you knew, he was being enlisted by a band of Romanies to reconnoiter a Spanish fort? Nothing was adding up, in this strange tale.

Rather than ask any of these questions, Geordie decided to ask a different one. "Why would they allow a prisoner to get married, in the first place? The Spanish aren't known for coddling prisoners—if it's information they want, they'll just torture it out of him."

Marcello explained, "They need the bridegroom's cooperation—he has a skill that is very useful to them, and this is why they indulge him." The man paused, and then added, "And I will admit that you have a skill we would find very useful, in turn. I understand you have knowledge of Congreve's rockets."

Hearing this, Adao caught his breath.

CHAPTER 8

Into the silence, Geordie admitted, "I do know a fair bit about the rockets. I'd an interest, and so I worked with the artillery, testing them out so as to improve them."

Congreve's rockets were a fairly recent invention in warfare; while flying bombs filled with black powder had been used for centuries, William Congreve had invented a type of "rocket" that could be accurately launched from a long distance away, but didn't require a cumbersome, heavy wooden frame to make its launch. These portable rockets were still being perfected–as many a man who'd lost a finger could attest–and Geordie, who was mechanical by nature, had been fascinated by them. And, because this new type of weapon would give its users an immense advantage, there was necessarily a great deal of secrecy involved in the attempts to perfect their use.

It seemed that the plan, here, was finally taking shape; the British couldn't move openly, and so instead, they were sending the gypsies into the Alcazar, using the wedding as an excuse. However, they needed someone with an expertise to accompany them, so as to reconnoiter the interior for a potential long-range rocket attack. Which was all very well and good, but at present there wasn't a war going forward, and Geordie decided that he may as well mention this troublesome fact. "Who's going to be shooting rockets inside the Alcazar? It's peace-time."

"We seek only to be prepared," Marcello offered smoothly, "for when the next war breaks out."

Geordie nodded, since this was plausible. The British must be worried about this particular fortification—and what was going on, within it—but they couldn't take any overt action, because they'd signed a peace treaty, and delicate negotiations were still ongoing. This must be the reason that the Army couldn't approach Geordie openly with such an assignment—hence these gypsies, and their wedding-party story.

Although—although, there was yet another hitch, that didn't make sense; surely there were men better-suited than Geordie, for this task? It seemed a little strange, that they'd gone to these convoluted lengths to recruit him, instead of one of the more experienced artillery rocketeers, many of whom were still stationed here in Spain.

Adao could contain himself no longer, and eagerly asked, "Can you show me how to make the rockets, *gadjo*?"

The boy's voice was filled with all the excitement that any stripling would have for such a prospect, but Geordie cautioned, "They're mighty dangerous, lad, and it's no easy task. To begin with, you need a decent metalworker, to put the shell casing together."

"I worked in metals with my father—I can learn," Adao insisted, and Geordie noted that Minos threw him a cautioning glance.

"If we've time," Geordie temporized, and then stood up, and made a show of stretching out his arms. "And now, if you'll excuse me, I'll want to check on my lass."

Hiding a smile at this private jest, he wandered over to sit on the stool that had been vacated by Adao, next to Etta. For a few moments he sat in silence beside the girl, as they watched the black mare munch on her bucket of oats.

In a quiet undertone, Geordie asked, "What's Adao to you?"

Etta kept her gaze on the horse, and replied evenly, "Adao is my brother."

"Try again," he said, almost kindly.

She glanced at him, her brows raised in surprise. "You don't believe me?"

"No." He smiled, to show he didn't hold it against her.

"You must pretend it is true," she whispered in an urgent undertone, as her gaze returned to the horse. "Please."

This was of interest, and as he reached to better position Jenny's bucket, he asked quietly, "Do they hold you against your will?" He didn't have that impression, but she may have decided she'd no choice but to be docile.

"No, I come willingly," she said, and offered nothing more.

Geordie weighed the chances of ever having another private conversation with her, and decided it was time to get down to the nub of it. "Here's the thing, lass; I will love you 'till the day I die, and I'm going to do my damnedest to break you out of this marriage contract. We'll go fishing on the river Tweed, and I'll teach you to bake scones, like my mother used to."

He let out a breath, and glanced up to find that she was staring at him, shocked, and then those grass-green eyes lit up with humor—Lord alive, but she was a bonny, bonny lass.

"You are far too impetuous, Captain," she whispered in a chiding tone. "How can you believe anything I've told you?"

"Oh, I know you're lying to me," he replied easily. "But I can overlook it."

"I am betrothed," she scolded in a severe tone, her eyes still alight. "You seek to dishonor me, I think."

"Oh, you've no idea," he returned, with a great deal of meaning.

"Etta?" Marcello called out. "Would you like more soup?"

"If there is more to be had," she agreed in a mild tone, and Marcello refilled her bowl, and then settled on the straw next to them.

Geordie didn't mind having a chaperone, since he'd managed to declare himself, and the lass hadn't immediately hit him with the joint-stool—a good sign, all in all.

"A fine mare," Marcello offered. "How did you come by her?"

"The Battle of Badajoz," Geordie replied, reaching out with affection to pat the glossy neck, that was stretched out before them. "Her rider had been unseated, and I was in sore need of a mount."

"You've had her, ever since then?" Marcello nodded in admiration. "She is in good condition, for such a history."

"Aye, that. I saw plenty of action with this doughty lass; she's as steady as they come, and never faltered—not even in hand-to-hand, with swords flashing on all sides. Faster than anything else on four hooves, too; I won many a wager from the other officers."

He paused, because he'd the sense that the others had suddenly stilled, and there was a long silence, within the room. He was recalled to the fact that everyone else seemed to be without a horse to their name, and so perhaps he shouldn't be boasting—not to mention that the gypsies were notorious horse thieves; best change the subject.

In a brisk tone, he asked, "Tell me, do we approach the Alcazar outright? If what you tell me is true, they'll not welcome a British soldier, within."

Marcello nodded. "Yes—a good point, and one which has been taken into consideration. You will be disguised, of course."

Geordie tilted his head. "I'm to pass as a Romany?" This seemed a little optimistic, as Geordie was the very picture of a big, bluff Scotsman, and the Romanies tended to be dark-haired, small and wiry. Except for Marcello, who—unless Geordie very much missed his guess—was more a relative to Etta than Adao was, although why this deception had been deemed necessary was not at all clear.

Marcello offered a dry smile. "You are to pass as the priest."

Geordie lifted his head to stare at him. "A *Papist* priest?"

The other man nodded. "Yes. It is the religion of our people."

Running a hand over his face, Geordie could see the wisdom in such a disguise—less suspicion would attach, if a priest were to be nosing around the Spanish fortification—besides, if he was to wear one of those long cassocks, mayhap he could smuggle-in a weapon, just to be safe. He shrugged in concession. "Aye then, I'll do it. But don't you dare tell anyone back at the kirk in Melrose."

"They will not hear of it from me," Marcello agreed.

CHAPTER 9

*S*ince the rain had been reduced to a light patter, they resumed their journey toward the gypsy camp, thinking that the weather would aid them in avoiding the notice of others. Etta was mounted again on Jenny, her shawl wrapped tightly around her, with the men casually walking alongside, hoping to give off the impression of travelers with nothing more important on their minds than the upcoming wedding celebration.

Marcello had stepped forward to help Etta mount, and then had offered to lead Jenny, which Geordie accepted with good grace, because the poor man was unaware that there was nothing to be done; the girl was destined for bonny Scotland, will-he or nil-he.

Geordie walked along with the others, but he'd decided that it would be prudent to strike up another conversation with Minos; there were still a couple of things that didn't add up, and hopefully he could get the funny little fellow talking again.

To this end, he shortened his strides so that he fell behind Marcello and Gaston, and out of earshot. "Which is your tribe, Minos? The bride's or the bridegroom's?"

"The bridegroom's," his companion replied, and, with a nod of his head, he included Gaston in his response. "The bridegroom is Gaston's brother, and I am his cousin."

Geordie lifted his face to consider the trees overhead. "You forgot that you told me you didn't know the bridegroom."

"I may lie to you," Minos admitted, with all appearance of regret. "It is the way of the *Rom*; it is how we survive."

"So; why is your cousin being held at the Alcazar? What's he done?"

It was clear that his companion debated what to tell him, before he disclosed, "It is more what he will not do, *gadjo*. He is being held there, because he will not cooperate."

Geordie raised his brows. "The Spanish are known to have ways to force cooperation, friend; there's more to this story."

"*Si, gadjo*," Minos agreed placidly, and offered nothing further.

They walked for a few paces, and then Geordie asked, "How much do the other Romanies—the ones we will meet in the camp, ahead–how much do they know about the plan? If they think I'm truly a priest, I should act the part."

With an easy gesture, his companion shrugged. "You

should always assume the *Rom* know everything, *gadjo*. Again, it is how we survive."

Geordie nodded. "Fair enough. I will count on you to give me warning, though, if anyone is planning to shiv me between the ribs."

Minos glanced up at him in amusement. "Do not worry, *gadjo*. No one would dare."

"Because I have a useful talent, like the bridegroom does." This was a shrewd guess; if the bridegroom merely held valuable information, it would have been extracted long ago. But if this Frenchman—Rochon—was willing to humor his captive by bringing him his chosen bride, then the prisoner must be useful to them in some other way. Taking a cast, Geordie asked, "Does the bridegroom know how to make rockets?"

"No," said Minos, as he glanced back at Adao, who was walking behind them. "It was Adao's father, who knew."

Apparently, Adao had been eavesdropping, and the boy now broke into their conversation without a qualm. "But my father would not show me; he said I was too young, and it was too dangerous."

Geordie could hear the pent-up frustration in the lad's voice, and said, not unkindly, "He'd the right of it. I've seen a more than a few killed, or come away without a hand, for their troubles."

"I will be careful," the boy insisted. "I wish to learn."

It had already occurred to Geordie that this might not be the best idea—to allow the Romany tribes to have the means to fire rockets at will—and so he temporized, "If it's possible, lad. It's not something you can put together out of sticks and mud, after all."

Minos gave Adao a glance, and the boy made no further protest. Nevertheless, Geordie felt a tug of sympathy for the lad; he'd probably watched the war's devastation, but was too young to fight—or help his father, who'd been covertly aiding the British. It seemed evident that his father was no longer alive, which made sense, since Etta was now the Queen. Although—come to think of it–shouldn't Adao have inherited his father's honors, and become the new *Rom Baro*? It was odd, that the tribal leadership would shift to whichever man managed to marry Etta, and since Geordie fully intended to marry the lass, himself, this raised a grave concern; the last needful thing was for him to be crowned King of the Gypsies.

But of course, he was thinking logically, and forgetting that he should not assume that any of them were what they said they were. For example, he'd already confirmed his suspicion that Etta and Adao were not related—the lad was a bit too tongue-tied around a girl who was supposedly his sister. And he'd be very much surprised if Minos was indeed related to Gaston, which also meant that he shouldn't believe anything they told him about the bridegroom, either. All in all, it raised some very troubling questions about why such deceptions—about who was who—were deemed necessary.

Mentally, he shrugged. He'd be wary, in his dealings with them, and in the end, it hardly mattered; Etta was going to marry no one save himself—so long as he could convince her of this, and he'd a feeling he was half-way there. The Romanies would have to struggle on as best they could, same as they'd done for hundreds of years. The war had devastated them, but the war had devastated everyone; it was a shame, but there it was, and no fixing it, anytime soon.

"May I watch you put the rockets together?" the boy asked again, unable to stay quiet. "I would very much like to watch."

"No one's putting any rockets together," Geordie said in some surprise. "It's peace-time."

Out of the corner of his eye, Geordie thought he saw another cautioning glance, directed toward the lad by Minos, and Adao immediately amended, "No—I meant, if you could please explain it to me, *gadjo*."

Geordie fell back into step beside the boy, and advised, "Fah, laddie; the rockets are a powerful weapon, and they mustn't fall into the wrong hands—it's always a race, to stay one step ahead of the enemy. I've got to be careful, for fear you'll run amok, like a berserker swinging a club."

Adao laughed, and Geordie laid an affable hand on the nape of his neck, processing the interesting fact that Adao seemed to be taking direction from Minos, who was supposedly from a distant tribe. Not to mention there was the lad's alarming slip about a rocket attack being in the works, despite the general ceasefire order. What did it mean? Did they think they could somehow force Geordie to make rockets, so as to aid a gypsy war? If that was indeed the plan, it all seemed a bit far-fetched—not to mention that they obviously didn't know Geordie very well, at all.

He kept these thoughts to himself, however, and cuffed the back of the boy's head with affection. "A Scot can appreciate a thirst for vengeance, lad—none better— but let's not burn everything down, in the process."

"Wise words, *gadjo*," Minos agreed, and then they all lapsed into companionable silence.

CHAPTER 10

The gypsy camp was situated on a meadow near the forest's edge, about a half-mile inland from the river. Two wooden caravan wagons were parked next to a campfire site, which was sheltered by a small tarp, hung between the wagons.

It was late afternoon when Geordie's party arrived, and they'd obviously been scouted, since a Romany man came forward to greet them as they approached, spreading his hands as he spoke in English. "Welcome, my brothers."

The men from Geordie's party came forward, one by one, to ceremoniously greet the man with a kiss on each cheek, murmuring salutations in the Romany language.

Beneath his patient demeanor, Geordie was suddenly wary, and carefully surveyed the encampment. He didn't like this—these cordial greetings; everyone seemed to be trying a little too hard, as though they were putting on a play.

"And you are the Englishman." The man smiled, and offered his hand. "Welcome; I am Tornys."

"Scotsman," Geordie corrected, and affably took the man's hand. "And if I'm to pose as a priest, someone had best explain the basics to me, before I give the game away."

"In time, in time," Tornys assured him, as he gestured toward the fire. "First, you must eat, and rest from your journey."

Marcello stepped forward to lift Etta down from her perch, and Adao offered to turn Jenny out into the makeshift rope-corral that was adjacent to the camp, where the draft horses cropped at the lush grass.

"Shouldn't we hobble her?" asked Tornys. "We wouldn't want her to escape."

"She won't take a hobble," Geordie explained. "But don't worry; she's not one to wander off."

Tornys nodded, and then turned to lead them over to the fire, where a woman was tending a kettle of stew, the kettle surrounded by medallions of flat-bread, baking on the stones around the fire. Upon their approach, the woman straightened up. "Welcome, Queen Etta," she said in a respectful tone. "I am Sasha, and I will help you prepare for your wedding."

"Thank you, Sasha," said Etta, and then she settled on a proffered stool near the fire, her gaze downcast, and her hands folded demurely on her lap.

Geordie, who'd been watching the interactions between these people, and drawing his own conclusions, offered in a casual tone, "Not a lot of guests, for such an important wedding." He decided not to ask how one man had managed to drive the two gypsy caravans.

With a gesture of regret, Tornys explained, "Yes—it is a shame that both the tribes cannot attend, but we wish to draw as little attention as possible. And we haven't much choice, in any event; the Comandante will allow only the bride, her menfolk, and the priest to enter the Alcazar. Indeed, we are fortunate they will allow the ceremony at all."

Geordie smiled his thanks at Sasha, as she handed him a bowl. "I suppose once the bridegroom is set free, your tribe can travel to Madrid, and celebrate with all the others."

"Indeed; that is what we plan," Tornys agreed in a hearty tone. "We hope to hurry the day—there will be much cause to celebrate."

The Romany man then turned to address Marcello. "If you would spare me a moment, good brother, I should tell you of the arrangements for the ceremony, tomorrow."

"Of course," said Marcello, and the two men retreated for a small distance, to confer in low voices—probably to make certain they'd got their story straight. Geordie had noted that Minos smiled into his bowl, when Geordie mentioned Madrid as the origin of Etta's tribe; apparently the little man appreciated a fellow trickster.

Geordie was then to hide his own smile, because as soon as Marcello was otherwise occupied, Etta took the opportunity to slide over beside him, on the pretext of reaching for the ladle. Willingly, he refilled her bowl for her, and then offered her his hearth bread, explaining, "I can't eat this myself, what with my tooth out. I'm that eager to find someone who can mend it up."

There was a moment of dismayed silence, as she lifted the proffered flatbread from his hand. "Perhaps you don't need your tooth, Captain," she ventured. "The gap is hardly noticeable."

Geordie bent to address his bowl of stew. "No, lass; I've only to find an apothecary, and he'll fix it up, right and tight."

"I am not certain that it can be fixed," she explained gently.

He paused to look at her in surprise. "No? I do have some horseshoe nails; I can try hammering it back in myself, I suppose."

There was a small silence, and then the laughter came up in her eyes. "You are teasing me. *Shame* on you."

He shrugged, and continued to chew thoughtfully. "I didn't want to tell you the true reason I kept it, which is that I'm going to find the fellow who knocked it out, and make him swallow it." He paused, and then explained, "Scots live for vengeance." May as well let her know what she was getting into; she didn't strike him as a shy flower, which was a good thing, all in all.

"I see," she said, lifting her eyebrows as she considered this.

"Measured vengeance," he corrected, just so she didn't think he was completely uncivilized. "I'll not kill him, because he didn't kill me."

"That is very generous of you," she replied.

There was something in her tone—some nuance—that gave him pause; it was as though she was very much amused, behind her thoughtful expression. Cocking his head, he continued to address his stew, but said in a serious tone, "Tell me straight-out what it is you're thinking, lass. Because I may be fair besotted, but I'd rather not be having to second-guess my wife at every turn—let's start out as we mean to go on."

Her eyes alight, she reminded him, "You speak nonsense, Captain; I will be wed to another, by this time tomorrow."

"Geordie," he paused to inform her with a smile. "My name is Geordie. And no, you'll not; not if I'm to act as the priest."

"That is a very good point," she agreed, as though much struck.

"What's afoot?" he repeated. "Or can't you tell me?"

"I can't tell you," she readily admitted.

"Any stew left?" Marcello asked in an overly-hearty tone, as he sat down on Geordie's other side.

"Plenty, friend," Geordie replied easily, and ladled-out a bowl. Someday soon, he'll have all the time he needed to speak with the lass, but that day was not today. Small matter; he was a patient man, and he still had to find out who was who, because he'd be very much surprised if anyone here was who they'd said they were.

Marcello took up his spoon, and informed them, "We have been given permission to hold the wedding tomorrow, in the late afternoon."

"Good—we've some time to prepare," said Geordie. "Someone's got to train me for my role."

Tentatively, Marcello suggested, "We are hoping you

will speak as little as possible, Captain. Although your Spanish is good, I'm afraid your accent gives you away."

Geordie paused his spoon and asked with mock-surprise, "Wha' accent? 'Tis you lot, what's got tha mingin' accent."

"Indeed," Marcello said with a small smile. "Nonetheless."

"I could pretend to be Irish," Geordie offered thoughtfully. "That would be more in keeping, for a Papist priest, and the Spanish wouldn't much know the difference."

"Excellent, if you can manage it." Marcello then nodded in the direction of Tornys, who'd sat down opposite them to take his meal. "We will do our planning in the wagons, so as to arouse no suspicions. The women will sleep in one wagon, and the men in the other."

"I wouldn't know what to do, with a roof over my head," Geordie explained easily. "I'll sleep here on the ground, beside the fire." Not to mention that he didn't trust a single one of them not to shiv him in the ribs, and then steal his Jenny, for good measure.

Although—although mayhap that wasn't exactly fair. He didn't think Marcello or Adao meant him any harm—or Minos, either, although he might well be foolish, to think he could trust any one of them. There was no question that everyone was keeping secrets from him—even the bonny lass, although at least she was willing to admit it.

Still and all, he truly didn't believe he was in any immediate danger, although he didn't have a good read on Gaston, as yet. The Brittany Romany seemed to be keeping himself to himself—didn't interact with the others, much—and Geordie wouldn't be surprised if the man craved a drink; he recognized the signs. In fact, Geordie had the impression Gaston wished he were anywhere but here, which seemed a little strange, if his brother was the bridegroom, and slated to be the next *Rom Baro*. Mayhap the two men didn't get along.

And then there was Tornys, who was yet another Romany who seemed to be play-acting a part—not to mention the man must have more support, than what was apparent. All in all, it would be prudent for Geordie to do a bit more probing, before he settled down to sleep in such company.

To this end, he squinted up at the twilight sky for a moment. "I'll want to take a reconnoiter, before I bed down," he remarked to Marcello. "Mayhap we could take a turn around the perimeter, you and me."

"Willingly," Marcello replied, and rose to his feet.

CHAPTER 11

The two men walked into the trees just as the last sunlight was fading over the hills, causing the valley to turn sepia-colored. It all seemed very peaceful, but Geordie knew better; in fact, if it weren't for the lass, he'd be tempted to whistle to Jenny and steal away at the first opportunity. As it was, however, he should do his best to curry favor with Marcello, who was ably hiding his concern that bonny Etta was falling for an uncivilized Scotsman.

As the two men walked side-by-side, Geordie began, "Perhaps you will be kind enough to tell me who you are, exactly, and what your purpose is."

Marcello looked over in surprise. "I don't understand."

"To start with, I don't think you're a Romany."

There was a pause whilst they walked in silence, the sunset breeze stirring the trees overhead. "What makes you think this, Captain?"

Geordie ran a practiced eye around his surroundings, and found nothing to alarm him. "Just a feeling."

The other man reviewed the ground before him, and slowly replied, "I will agree that all is not as it appears, but I assure you, we seek your services in good faith."

"I'll be the judge o' that, I think," Geordie replied. "Can you give me a glimpse, at least?"

The other man thought about it for a moment, and then nodded. "There are several purposes being served, here; the Queen will indeed be delivered to the prisoner, and the wedding will serve as an excuse for a reconnaissance mission—to reconnoiter the Alcazar's interior." He paused. "I will confess that I have every intention of planning a rocket attack on this facility. However, I would like to destroy only those areas that are housing weapons and supplies, as opposed to housing soldiers, or civilians. This is why I have asked for your help, in determining how best this can be accomplished."

Geordie cocked a skeptical brow. "You're willing to wage an attack, but you want to spare the soldiers?"

Marcello nodded. "I do. Most of the soldiers here are Spaniards, who have been forced to serve the *Afrancesados*, who now rule Spain. They are only following their orders, and don't deserve to be slaughtered."

Geordie nodded, seeing the wisdom of this strategy— if the soldiers' loyalty did not lie with those in charge, they may not be overly-concerned with pursuing the attackers who'd been careful to spare their lives. "Aye, then; but I don't think you've answered my question, friend. Whose interest do you represent, and why would you want to attack the Alcazar?"

Marcello considered his answer. "My interests are opposed to Napoleon's interests, which is why we are monitoring the situation, here."

Geordie made a sound of impatience, and spread his hands. "Lord alive—why is everything such a secret? It makes me leery; I'll not be working against the interests of the British Army."

His companion immediately lifted his head, and assured him, "No—you wouldn't be; my word on it. And please believe me, when I tell you that I don't wish to wage a war; instead, I only seek to cripple Napoleon's operations, here."

Geordie asked outright, "Are you a spy, for the British?"

"No," Marcello replied, unruffled by the question. "Although often we have the same objectives."

He offered nothing further, and Geordie wasn't sure whether or not to believe him. Geordie had been recruited by the British spymaster once, himself—although he'd turned the man down—and it seemed to him that Marcello was just the right sort of candidate for that type of covert work. In fact, he wouldn't have been at all surprised to discover that Marcello was indeed spying for the British, and therefore could not begrudge the man for being so careful with his information.

Instead of pressing him, Geordie asked, "Tell me about Tornys."

"You may trust Tornys," Marcello assured him.

"As far as you know," Geordie added, with a touch of irony.

His companion nodded in reluctant acknowledgement. "Many personnel choices are not my own," he offered, rather obliquely. "But we do share the same objectives."

As this seemed yet another veiled response to a forthright question, Geordie made no comment, and they walked for a few moments in silence, which seemed to prompt Marcello to decide he should impart a bit more information. "Napoleon's people have need of the bridegroom, and they are trying to bribe him into aiding their cause. They must bribe him with something other than money, however, because there is a wealthy Englishman who is, in turn, bribing him to help the British, and Napoleon's people cannot outspend the Englishman."

Geordie tilted his head thoughtfully. "So, the bridegroom has demanded that he be wed to the Gypsy Queen, so as to set himself up as the Gypsy King."

"Yes."

Geordie eyed him sidelong. "The bridegroom, who is Gaston's brother."

Marcello nodded, unsurprised that Geordie had discovered this. "Yes. The bridegroom's name is Gerard. The two brothers are Brittany Romanies."

Geordie nodded, as it seemed that he was finally— more or less—finding a kernel of truth, hidden away amongst all the misdirection and sleight-of-hand. It was interesting that Marcello was not willing to admit that he wasn't a Romany, even though he was willing to admit that his goal was to destroy the Alcazar, and Geordie took a good guess as to why this was. If Marcello admitted he was not a Romany, then Geordie might be led to realize that Etta was not a Romany, either, and that this entire Gypsy Queen wedding story was a sham—merely an excuse to get them within the fortification.

The poor man didn't know that Geordie had already figured this out, of course, and so he decided it would be best to keep his conclusions to himself, until he discovered why everyone seemed to think that such an elaborate charade was necessary—and why Geordie, of all people, had been recruited into this implausible plot.

Yet again, the only reason Geordie could think of seemed to be the obvious one—the bridegroom wanted to pass along information to him. It was the only thing that made sense; Geordie had been asking questions about Colonel Merryfield's death, had got beat-up for his troubles, and now he'd landed thick in the midst of people who must know the truth about what happened to the Colonel. It couldn't *possibly* be a coincidence.

Keeping these rather hopeful thoughts to himself, Geordie decided to cut to the nub of the mystery. "And why is the bridegroom so valuable? Can you tell me?"

They walked a few steps further, and then Marcello decided to explain, "Gerard is a skilled counterfeiter. Rochon—who is Napoleon's spymaster—is desperate; there is talk that a lucrative counterfeiting operation has been interrupted, and they must now persuade Gerard to create new counterfeiting plates, and as quickly as possible. It is not something that can be forced, however, and time is of the essence."

Geordie raised his brows, and thought this over. "I'd heard rumor that Napoleon took to producing counterfeit coins, toward the end of the war."

Marcello nodded. "Yes; the paper money is of no value, anymore—France's treasury is empty, and everyone knows it. Napoleon cannot attempt another war without the funding for it, and so he is reduced to counterfeiting the money that he will need."

Geordie nodded, and decided not to press his companion further. The man was going to be kin, after all, and so he probably shouldn't wonder aloud why—if Marcello was supposedly working to oppose Napoleon's counterfeiting plans—he was willing to deliver-up the very bribe which would allow exactly that. There was more to it, of course; as Geordie himself had pointed out, Etta wasn't marrying anyone, if Geordie was to be posing as the priest.

Perhaps the Romanies were going to smuggle-in something to Gerard, so as to help him escape? This, however, seemed a very convoluted tack to take; it would be far easier to bribe a guard, or a servant. There were too many layers, here—too many cooks, making this meal, and it all made little sense to him.

With this in mind, Geordie admitted, "I'm not easy about this. I'm playing blind man's bluff, and I canno' say I like it much."

"And there is no blame to you, Captain," Marcello agreed. "But I am afraid I am not at liberty to tell you more."

Geordie met his eyes. "Tell me this, then; how can you be certain the Romanies aren't part of the counterfeiting operation, and that you're not the one being hoodwinked? After all, gypsies would be well-placed, to pass along false coins."

Marcello replied in an even tone, "You presume I am not a Romany, myself."

"I beg your pardon," Geordie said a bit ironically, and held his peace. The reason he'd asked the question was because it had suddenly occurred to him that a gambling-den was an excellent place to pass along counterfeit coins, if you wished to conceal their origin, and— coincidentally enough—a gambling-den was where Colonel Merryfield had been killed, right after that smoky Romany fellow had started hanging about.

Not to mention that the counterfeit coins would no doubt be silver, and—as a further coincidence—the Colonel had quietly given Geordie the mortgage to his silver mines in Sheffield, England. When the Colonel had given the document to him—for safekeeping, he'd said— his commander had hinted strongly that Geordie should consider marrying his daughter, since she'd be the one to inherit the mines.

And so, after the Colonel was killed, Geordie had dutifully offered for the lass—she wasn't yet of age, but she'd no one else, and it seemed appropriate, under the circumstances. She'd turned him down, which was just as well, since she'd have been a handful for any man, and didn't know the first thing about fishing.

But now—now, Geordie held the mortgage to silver mines in Sheffield—of all places—and was presented with a puzzle that seemed to be slowly getting itself pieced together. Because he was forthright by nature, it was on the tip of his tongue to make mention of all this to Marcello–to warn him, in the event he didn't realize the scope of what was afoot–but he drew back; again, best keep his own counsel, for the time being. With any luck, he'd sort out who-was-who, stymie Napoleon's operations in Spain, clear the Colonel's good name, and gain a bonny bride, to boot.

CHAPTER 12

As Geordie continued his walk around the camp's perimeter with Marcello, he turned his attention to more practical matters. "Who's in the wedding party? Aside from you and me."

"Gaston will attend, to stand up with his brother at the ceremony. Minos–who is a cousin to them, and Adao, along with you and me."

Geordie tilted his head in mild disagreement. "Is it wise to bring-in Adao? If the lad's father died in the war, he may not behave himself, in the company of the *Afrancesados*. He may be champing for a bit o' vengeance."

"It is important that the boy be present for the ceremony," Marcello explained. "His father was *Rom Baro*, and if his father's son participates, it will help to solidify Gerard's claim, and bring unity to the tribes."

Thus reminded, Geordie asked, "Why isn't Adao the *Rom Baro* outright, then? Because he's but a lad?"

Marcello glanced up at the sky, where the stars were now starting to appear, one by one. "It is not so simple, Captain; in Romany tradition, leadership is determined through the Queen."

"That's a strange way of doing things," Geordie was compelled to say. "Although I suppose it means the leadership gets spread out amongst good candidates, instead of being kept to one family."

"Exactly," Marcello agreed.

Geordie cocked his head. "Although it also means the Queen herself is put at risk for a kidnapping—just like what happened here; with the attempt on Etta."

"Yes," Marcello agreed, in an even tone. "It is a problem, indeed."

The poor man doesn't realize that Minos is the weak link, thought Geordie, *and so I already know it was all a sham. Ah well—he's doing his best, and I don't think he enjoys having to dupe me; at least, not as much as Minos does.*

They turned to head back toward the camp, and Geordie asked, "So; you think the lad will behave himself, and follow orders? And the others, too?"

"I do."

Geordie offered bluntly, "You may be overly hopeful, friend. Everyone's swimming in secrets, and Minos has all but admitted the Romanies lie for a living."

Marcello contemplated the ground for a few moments, apparently still unwilling to admit to Geordie that he wasn't, in fact, a Romany. "We march with the army we have, Captain. I have confidence they will do as I ask, mainly because there is no love for either the French or the Spanish amongst the Romany people, and the idea of taking part in an attack is very appealing to them."

"Not to mention they'd like their kinsman out of prison, in one piece."

Marcello bowed his head. "That, too."

Geordie decided to change the subject, being as Marcello was proving to be nearly as stubborn as Geordie, which was truly saying something. "Can you tell me of Adao's father—the old *Rom Baro*? I understand he helped the British, during the war."

Marcello glanced up at the starry sky. "A very brave man. He was a skilled metal-worker, and pretended to aid the French by working in the Armory at Arlabán. He fashioned armaments, and worked on rockets with the hope of rivaling the British rockets. In truth, however, he was working for the British, and sabotaging Napoleon's efforts. Then one night, just before a battle, he opened the doors of the Armory to Spanish *guerrillas* so that they could set fire to the entire arsenal."

Geordie whistled softly. "I remember hearing about it —they say the sky was lit-up for miles."

"Yes—it was a great victory." His companion paused. "It came at a terrible cost, however. The French realized that Adao's father had collaborated with the *guerrillas*, and they promptly executed him. Then they killed nearly everyone in his tribe as punishment—to discourage other Romanies from taking sides against them. Adao survived by fleeing on his father's horse, even though he was but a small boy. The French still seek him, to this day."

"Ach, poor lad," said Geordie in sympathy. "But this

tale doesn't help me think that Adao will mind himself, once he's within the Alcazar."

"He will do as he's told," Marcello assured him, and Geordie felt he could raise no further protest; Marcello was no fool, and if he felt Adao's presence was necessary to give credence to the charade, then it must outweigh any potential hazard the boy might present.

They returned to the camp, where the others were in the process of banking the fire, and settling in for the night.

"I'll see to my horse," Geordie said to Marcello, and then strode over toward the makeshift corral, where Jenny was cropping at the grass, and didn't even bother to lift her head, at his approach. She seemed very content, and Geordie leaned against a tree and watched the mare for a moment, rather hoping that Etta would take the opportunity to come over to speak with him, again. He dared not approach her, not after noting that Marcello never once made mention of the lass, during their conversation. *She's kin to him,* he thought, *and he doesn't want me to figure that out. But Marcello and I are slated to be kin too, and so I should soothe him as best I can. With any luck, all his attempts to hoodwink me are for good reasons, and not for ill.*

Since it didn't seem as though Etta was going to emerge from the caravan, Geordie checked on Jenny's water, and then straightened up to turn back toward the camp. In the moonlight, he could see that Sasha lingered outside the women's wagon, her gaze meeting Geordie's in a subtle but familiar invitation. She was buxom and saucy, but he was no longer interested in buxom and saucy, and so with a polite smile of declination, he walked over to bed down beside the fire, and prepare to sleep as best he could. He'd need his wits about him tomorrow, if he was any judge of such things.

CHAPTER 13

Dawn was breaking when Geordie woke, his senses suddenly alert as his hand closed around the hilt of his pistol. Someone was approaching up the meadow, although it appeared to be an older man, carrying a bundle, and none too steady on his feet. Rising, Geordie held his pistol at the ready as the figure slowly approached; the visitor appeared harmless, but appearances could be deceiving.

Upon sighting Geordie, the man stopped short, eying him narrowly.

"Good morning, friend," said Geordie. "State your business."

The visitor regarded the pistol with open scorn, and drew his elderly frame upright. "You think to shoot me? I laugh at your pistol, *señor*; instead, you must ask how many times I was shot at Saragossa."

"How many times?" asked Geordie.

"Thrice," the man replied, in all defiance. "And I'd be

shot thrice more, just to see the Frenchman get his comeuppance."

"I don't know what you're talking about," said Geordie, hiding his dismay at this breach of security. "Explain yourself."

Ignoring Geordie's weapon, the man walked over to throw his bundle on the ground, and grasp a poker so as to stir-up the fire. "I'm to make you into a priest, sir. Have you anything to eat?"

Geordie lowered his pistol in surprise. "Lord alive; *you're* a Padre?"

The visitor pulled up a stool, and sat to warm his hands in the glowing embers. "You're to keep a civil tongue in your head, *señor*—not that I'd expect any less, from an *Ingles* heretic."

"Not *Ingles*," Geordie corrected. "*Escocés*, instead."

"Bah, even worse," the other declared sourly. "I could use a drink, if you've any to hand."

Geordie reached to pull up his own stool, and decided not to mention that it was a bit too early to start drinking, even for a Scotsman. "I've not, I'm afraid."

With a grunt of disappointment, the priest glanced up at the silent wagons. "The *mujer dejada* should be up, soon. She'll see to me."

This, said with a sidelong gleam, and Geordie could only wonder how the man managed to remain a clergyman, since he seemed to foster more than a few unholy habits. On the other hand, the bravery of the priests at Saragossa was legendary; the battle between the Spanish and Napoleon's forces had raged for months, with massive losses to both sides when it was finally over.

"Have you been within the walls of the Alcazar, Padre?" Geordie decided that he may as well ask, it seemed clear the elderly man had been advised of the plan, and Geordie could use any information he could glean.

"Many times," his companion replied, and then sucked on his gums thoughtfully. "You've bad luck, because a prisoner escaped from here—a few weeks ago —and as a result, there are more guards than the usual." He fixed his rheumy eyes on Geordie, and added, "It caused quite a stir, and the Frenchman was very unhappy —got himself wounded, trying to get his prisoner back, but no luck to him." He then paused to cackle, thinking on this with a great deal of satisfaction.

Geordie reached down to brush aside some leaves from the packed dirt beneath their feet, and handed his companion a stick. "Can you map-out the layout for me?"

With a shrug, the man took up the stick, but advised, "I'm not familiar with the whole of it; I deliver the Amontillado to the Comandante, and so I know mainly the route between the gate, and his quarters."

Geordie looked upon him with surprise. "You deliver his wine? Isn't that like asking a cat to deliver a mouse?"

"Hah!" The priest eyed him in amusement. "It is sacramental wine, delivered along the river-route to the priests in the area. It is a very fine vintage, and so I always take an extra cask or two, and deliver it up to the Comandante, here at the Alcazar. The man appreciates his fine wine." He paused, and then added piously, "In truth, I am a good Samaritan."

"For a price," said Geordie cynically.

"It is a very fine vintage," the priest defended himself.

Geordie shook his head. "And you're a very strange sort of priest."

"Since you've known so many," his companion countered with full scorn.

"Show me what you know about the layout," Geordie prompted, indicating the stick again. "Anything will help."

Dutifully, the older man began to scratch at the ground, but paused to look up at Geordie. "There's a girl within the Alcazar—Ines, her name is. She is a kitchen girl." He smacked his lips in appreciation. "She would be of help—she's familiar with every corner of the Alcazar, if you understand my meaning."

But Geordie cautioned, "I am not certain that Marcello wants too many to know about this wedding party."

Slyly, the man glanced up sidelong. "Marcello has his own interests, this is true. But as for me, I am certain that Ines can be trusted."

Geordie tilted his head toward him. "Tell me of Marcello's interests."

Chuckling, the priest refocused on his map. "And how do I know that *you* can be trusted, *Escocés*?"

"You don't. But there must be some reason Marcello wants me tangled-up in all this, and damned if I know what it is."

The old man nodded in agreement. "*Si*; these people, they'd rather you weren't here at all. It is the bridegroom who seeks you out, and everyone must do as he asks."

Geordie made no comment, since he was unwilling to admit that he'd already been told as much. Until he understood the lay of the land, he shouldn't assume that anyone could be trusted, and therefore he should carefully check everyone's story against all the other stories. But from what he'd gleaned, he had to agree with the priest; it was the bridegroom who'd insisted that Geordie be present, and—hopefully—that was because he wanted to pass along information. In fact, it was a good sign that the bridegroom was taking such pains to ensure secrecy; he must know something important.

The Padre continued, "Marcello has at least one man within the walls—a local surgeon. Tello, is his name."

Hearing this, Geordie frowned slightly, since Marcello himself hadn't told him this. "This Tello is not a Romany?"

"No. He spoke privately with Marcello, under the cover of the trees, after Marcello came here yesterday."

Geordie considered this, and concluded, "Marcello must be paying him for information."

The Padre shrugged his thin shoulders. "Perhaps. More likely, he brings information about the casket." Pausing, the older man slid his gaze over, and waited for Geordie's reaction.

Slowly, Geordie shook his head. "Not a clue, friend."

The priest bent his head, so as to continue with his scratching. "When the Frenchman returned here, with his wounded shoulder, and his foul temper, he brought with him a wooden casket, about this big." He paused, to indicate the size with his hands. "The Comandante tells me the casket is locked away in the Alcazar's Armory, and it is worth more than his life if anything happens to it —he mightily fears the Frenchman." In an aside, he paused to advise, "The Comandante speaks a little too freely, when he is in his cups."

Geordie prompted, "So; what's in the casket?"

The Padre shook his head. "The Comandante does not know. No one knows."

Geordie offered, "Except Marcello, you think."

"That's my guess," his companion agreed. "He does not seem like one who'd be mixed-up in this wedding business."

Since Geordie had come to this same conclusion on his own, he nodded thoughtfully. "Aye. Mayhap this casket contains gold? It will be needed, if Napoleon wants to ride again."

"I know not," the priest disclaimed, and spread his hands. "But I know this; the world would be a better place if the Frenchman did not have this casket. And if he were dead–that would be better, too."

In a mild tone, Geordie replied, "What you're suggesting would be in breach of the peace treaty, and so I will pretend I did not hear it."

"Soft, you are," the Padre scoffed. "Fah; you wouldn't have lasted a month, at Saragossa."

"We needed less than a week, at Badajoz," Geordie countered.

Impressed, the priest raised his sparse eyebrows, and grudgingly admitted, "At Badajoz, were you? Not so soft, then. But I will warn you to be wary, *Escocés*. Things are not what they seem."

"You're not the only one who's told me so," Geordie assured him.

CHAPTER 14

 arcello emerged from the wagon to join them, just as the sun's rays were breaking through the trees. "Good morning, Captain. I see you have met the Padre."

"I brought him a cassock," the priest explained, indicating the bundle. "It will be too short, but that can't be helped."

Marcello nodded, as he pulled up a stool to join them. "Yes. We may have to adjust our plan, Captain—we didn't anticipate your accent, I'm afraid. Tornys and I think it would be best if the Padre comes along with the wedding party. If anyone asks, we will explain that it is traditional to have a priest from both tribes, for such an important wedding. That way, you can speak as little as possible." He paused, and then added diplomatically, "I would advise you to pretend that you do not speak Spanish."

Geordie nodded willingly. "Aye, that would probably be for the best. And it will give me more freedom to

"

reconnoiter." He indicated the Padre's map, in the dirt. "I'm hoping to get a preliminary lay-out, so as to have a leg up."

Crouching down beside them, Marcello indicated with a finger. "We believe the Armory is here, located in the yard that is adjacent to the prisoner's cells. The bridegroom is not being held in the cells, however; instead he is being held in this outbuilding, near the officer's quarters." He pointed to it, and glanced up. "It is not the usual, and it is a mark of his value."

Geordie nodded. "And the barracks?"

"Over here," Marcello indicated.

"Good," said Geordie with a satisfied nod. "For a rocket attack, the Armory should be taken out first—it will scare the daylights out of everyone, and deprive them of munitions, at the same time. The building is isolated enough that you should be able to make an accurate strike, and keep the casualties to a minimum."

"Excellent," said Marcello. "Exactly as I'd hoped."

"You'll need a good metal worker, to fashion the rockets," Geordie warned. "A blacksmith, mayhap—someone who knows how to weld a tight seam. If the cannister isn't right, they'll misfire, and you're likely to lose more of your own men than theirs."

"We will have a good blacksmith," Marcello assured him.

Idly, Geordie tilted his head. "Have you any allies, within the walls? The Padre knows a kitchen girl; she would be well-placed to hear rumors. The side that's done the best reconnaissance usually wins the battle."

Smiling slightly, Marcello didn't answer the question,

but instead replied, "We do not anticipate a battle, Captain."

Geordie chuckled. "That's exactly what everyone says, just before the battle breaks out."

The Padre cackled, but then was distracted by Sasha, who'd come over to fetch the water bucket. The woman lingered to respond to the priest's flirtatious greeting, and Geordie took advantage of the interruption to rise and saunter over to check on Jenny, whistling to her as he came over to the side of the corral. The more he heard about the plan, the more uneasy he felt about his own role. He assumed the British were behind the planned attack on the fort—it only made sense—but he'd only Marcello's word for that, and there was no question that Marcello hadn't always been honest with him. It would probably be best if he not get too involved; no one liked a good bombardment better than Geordie, but he shouldn't let his enthusiasm land him in gaol, for breach of the peace.

He heard someone coming down the caravan's steps and looked up, hoping it was Etta, but instead of Etta, he was met with the sight of Gaston, emerging from the men's wagon.

In a friendly fashion, Geordie called out to him, "Ho, there; I hope there are no hard feelings, about your dunk in the river. I wasn't certain, at the time, whether you were friend or foe."

After the barest hesitation, Gaston came over to stand beside Geordie. "No; no harm done, *gadjo*."

Affably, Geordie continued, "I understand you're to stand up with the bridegroom, today."

"Yes." Again, there was the barest hesitation. "Gerard is my brother, *gadjo*."

Casually, Geordie ran a hand down Jenny's shoulder, as the horse reached her neck through the ropes, and began to snuffle at the newcomer. "What's the poor fellow being held for? Did he steal some wine from the Comandante?"

Gaston unbent enough to smile slightly, and then lifted a hesitant hand, to turn his palm to the horse's nose. "Perhaps. I have not spoken to him, in some time."

"Best mend fences, then–he's getting himself a bonny bride," Geordie said. "And if she's dripping in groats, all the better."

Gaston glanced at him. "Groats?"

"Money," Geordie explained patiently. "Which is quite a boon, nowadays. What do you know of her father, the *Rom Baro*? How did he manage to get himself a fortune?"

"In truth, he was foolish man," Gaston replied, an edge of bitterness to his tone. "The *Rom* have always stayed away from the *gadjo* wars; the *gadjo* cannot be trusted to treat the *Rom* fairly—everyone knows this." He paused, and then continued, "Adao's father worked with the Spanish *guerrillas* to help the British, and as a result, his tribe was wiped out–destroyed. It was only luck, that Adao wasn't killed, too; the *guerrillas* took him in, and hid him, which was the least they could do."

The other man subsided into silence, and Geordie made no comment, being as he'd gone through years of hardship and sacrifice as a soldier, and thus took a different view of things. It was a shame that the lad's father had died for his bravery, but plenty of other good men had died, too. And besides, if the Spanish *guerrillas* had recruited Adao's father, it was a mark of the man's merit; the *guerrilla* fighters were folk heroes, here in Spain —a group of ordinary citizens who'd banded together to harass and sabotage Napoleon's supply lines. They'd been so successful, with their tactics, that they'd actually turned the tide of the war. The *guerrillas* were legendary fighters who'd been willing to risk everything, as opposed to this poor fellow standing beside him, who apparently believed that nothing was worth such a risk.

Jenny sought out Gaston's hand again, and so tentatively, he reached to stroke the horse's nose.

Geordie offered, "You sound like someone who's weathered a betrayal or two, yourself."

"Yes," Gaston admitted, and offered nothing more. Straightening up, he pulled his hand away from Jenny. "I'm to fetch some eggs for breakfast." As he turned to go, he remarked over his shoulder, "You have a fine horse, *gadjo*."

"No point in stealing her," Geordie warned, only half-joking. "She's an escape artist, and she'll only come find me again."

With a thin smile, the other man walked away.

CHAPTER 15

After breakfast, Geordie recruited Minos to come with him to fish in the river. "We'll catch something fresh for lunch; I'm mighty tired of stew and soup."

The smaller man shrugged. "I do not have a fishing pole, *gadjo*."

"You can string the fish for me," Geordie said firmly. "Let's go."

Reconciled to his fate, the Romany man fell into step beside him, huffing a bit to keep pace with his larger companion. As they came to the river's edge, Geordie sought out a likely spot with a practiced eye—it would be good to fish again; his head was full of tangled thoughts, and there was nothing like casting a line over water to help sort them out. He was hoping he'd get Minos talking, again, now that he'd a clearer picture of what was afoot.

"Over here," Geordie advised, noting a shallow area

in the shadow of the trees. "The water's not running as fast, and the fish should be lurking."

"If you say, *gadjo*," Minos agreed, as he clambered over the roots and rocks after him.

Geordie unwound his drop-line, and then broke off a likely branch, to support the twine. As he swung his line out over the water, he remarked, "Are you looking forward to this wedding? I hope it speeds the day when your cousin is set free."

"Yes; me, too, *gadjo*," Minos agreed. "Gerard is tired of being held prisoner."

Geordie glanced at him. "When will they let him go, do you know?"

Minos shrugged. "Very soon—he has only to cooperate."

Geordie nodded. "It doesn't sound like he has much choice, but at least he'll get a bride, in the bargain. She has a handsome dowry, I understand."

"The tribe will be happy," Minos agreed. "It is very important, in these times."

This gave Geordie the opening he was looking for, and he remarked, "They tell me that Adao is coming along with us, into the Alcazar."

Minos nodded. "*Si*. They tell me the same."

Geordie adjusted his makeshift pole, moving his line in an attempt to inveigle any curious fish, who might be lurking around the hook. "Is that wise? The lad's got good reason to hold a grudge."

Idly, Minos plucked a piece of the tall grass that grew beside the rock he sat upon, and began to pull it apart. "The boy does not strike me as a hothead, *gadjo*."

"No," Geordie agreed, duly noting that Minos hadn't risen to the bait, and was going to pretend that he didn't know Adao, even though Geordie had the impression they knew each other very well. "And good for him; if I were his age, I'd have probably got myself killed by now, trying to take some sort of revenge."

"If you say," Minos replied doubtfully. "You do not strike me as a hothead, either, *gadjo*."

Since it seemed clear that Minos was not going to be drawn about the boy, Geordie tried a different approach. "Tell me of the lad's father—the *Rom Baro*."

The Romany man sighed with regret. "He was a clever tool-maker, and brought much wealth to his tribe."

Geordie made a sound of sympathy, as he watched his line with a discerning eye. "A shame, that he was killed. How did it happen?"

"He was caught in the town of Guarda, just as the siege began, and so he was killed, along with everyone else." Solemnly, the other man shook his head. "Bad luck, to be selling his wares in the wrong place, and at the wrong time."

Geordie readily agreed. "Aye—that's bad luck, indeed. And a shame, for such a good lad to lose his father so young. I knew a girl in the Army about his same age; her father survived the war, but then he was killed in a gambling-den, soon after." He shook his head ruefully, as he balanced on a tree root, and swung-out his lure again. "You can be as careful as you wish, but then fate has a way of catching up with you."

"It is of all things true," Minos agreed.

Geordie fished in silence for a few minutes, as the

river gurgled over the rocks, and the dragonflies buzzed along the shore. "I'm a plain man, Minos, and damned if I wish I could hear some plain-speaking, for a change."

Minos replied with great regret, "You may not get your wish, *gadjo*."

Geordie turned his head to regard him thoughtfully. "They don't need me, here—in fact, I am more a hindrance to this wedding than not. Marcello already has the lay of the land, and he doesn't need my help; he has his own sources. And I'm not the only ex-soldier around here with a knowledge of the rockets—in fact, I'm nowhere near as expert as some." He paused, and turned his gaze back over the water. "I'm inclined to think there is something else at play."

"There is," his companion affirmed, and then added almost apologetically, "But I am not likely to tell you."

Glancing at him in amused exasperation, Geordie shifted his makeshift pole. "For starters, I don't think everyone in our group is a Romany."

Geordie waited to see whether Minos would confirm this—it wasn't really necessary, of course; Gaston had confirmed it unwittingly, when he'd spoken of Adao's father, and Adao's close escape, but had never once mentioned Etta, the boy's supposed sister. It would be interesting, nevertheless, to test out Minos, and hear what he'd say.

To his surprise, the other man readily admitted, "This may be true, *gadjo*."

Slowly, Geordie shook his head. "I don't understand the need for the charade, and I'll confess it makes me uneasy."

But Minos didn't offer any insights, and instead asked in all curiosity, "If you are suspicious, *gadjo*, then why do you stay?"

Because Geordie was not about to admit to his own wedding plans–or delve into the particulars of Colonel Merryfield's death–he countered, "I'm not the only one who is suspicious, friend. It seems to me there are splintered factions, here—almost as many as there are people—with everyone mighty wary of the others, despite all their supposed brotherhood."

Minos nodded thoughtfully, as he watched the water. "This may be true, *gadjo*, and for the same reasons you said; sometimes fate takes a hand."

"There's some sort of treasure-casket in the Armory, I hear." Geordie thought he may as well say it; he thought it interesting that the Padre seemed to think this casket was Marcello's true aim, but Marcello had never once mentioned it to Geordie. Which wasn't much of a surprise, all in all; Marcello struck him as someone who played his cards very close to the vest.

Minos raised his grizzled brows in interest. "*Si*? Is it the royal treasure?"

It was Geordie's turn to raise his brows. "A *royal* treasure? Kept here at the Alcazar?"

The Romany man smiled at Geordie's skeptical reaction. "It does not seem likely, does it, *gadjo*? But there are rumors that the *guerrillas* were safeguarding the Spanish royal treasure, until Rochon seized it from them in Aranjuez, a few weeks ago."

Thinking this over, Geordie could only shake his head. "That's a hopeful tale, friend, but it's far too fanciful. The

British hold this territory, and they're not going to stand by whilst treasure is looted—they have eyes and ears everywhere. Besides, it's almost impossible to believe any sort of treasure wasn't looted long before now; everyone is desperate for money—even the *guerrillas*."

Minos tossed his piece of grass into the river, and watched it float away. "You speak the truth, *gadjo*. What is in the casket, then?"

"Gold?" Geordie speculated. "I'd say silver, but if this casket's so valuable, for that size it must be filled with gold."

Just then, Geordie felt a firm tug, and—with a sound of satisfaction—he whipped the makeshift pole to the side, so as to deposit a flopping fish onto the river bank.

"I will get it," Minos called out, and then clambered across the roots and outcroppings of rock to seize the fish, and remove the hook.

But if Minos was hoping this interruption would distract Geordie from his interrogation, he was to be disappointed, because as Geordie re-cast his line out over the water, he continued, "You tell me that fate has brought everyone together, but how? How did your cousin even know about this Gypsy Queen, if his tribe is not from hereabouts?"

"All the *Rom* know of the Gypsy Queen, *gadjo*—every last one of them," the other man replied, and it seemed to Geordie that Minos didn't necessarily think this was a good thing. "She is called the *Alkippa*, and is greatly revered."

With a knit brow, Geordie tried to make sense of it—if this tale was true, and a revered Gypsy Queen did indeed exist, it certainly wasn't Etta. Clearly, this wedding was a sham—that much was a given, even though Minos didn't want to admit as much. But time was short, and Geordie needed some answers, and so he decided he may as well take the bull by the horns. "Is your cousin being hoodwinked?" In the end, this seemed the only theory that held together; all these people must have an interest in delivering up a false Queen to the bridegroom, so as to provoke some unexplained benefit. But what was the benefit? Surely, they didn't wish for the man to go on counterfeiting for Napoleon?

Chuckling, Minos plucked another piece of tall grass. "No, *gadjo*. Instead, it is you, who is being hoodwinked." He paused, apparently thinking about this with great amusement.

This had the ring of truth, and Geordie warned in an ominous tone, "I'll not walk into danger, friend."

Minos nodded in ready agreement. "This is very clear to me. And it makes me wonder why you do."

Geordie's mouth twisted with amusement at the other man's boldness, but decided to admit, "I am looking for answers. A friend was killed."

Minos glanced over at him. "The girl's father? The one you mentioned?"

In an even tone, Geordie replied, "I'll not give you answers, if you'll not give me answers."

"Fah, *gadjo*; I have already given you plenty of answers," Minos protested. "My word as a *Rom*."

"Do you know anything of it—of my friend's death?" For a moment, Geordie teetered on the edge of offering a bribe for information, but drew back. Despite all appearances, he didn't have the sense that Minos was someone who could be bribed. "Do you have any information as to who killed him, and why?"

As he watched Geordie's fishing line, Minos shrugged. "Maybe yes, maybe no. But first, we must bring the Gypsy Queen to the bridegroom."

"Aye, then," Geordie agreed, thinking he'd his own reasons to seek out the bridegroom. "First things, first, but then I'll be much obliged if you'll tell me what you know."

"First things, first," Minos agreed.

CHAPTER 16

It was noon-time, and Geordie was eating the fish that they'd caught, along with all the other men. Sasha was waiting on them, serving up watered ale so to make the day-old hearth-cakes more palatable.

Geordie hadn't caught a glimpse of Etta, so far this day, and he was starting to wonder if perhaps she was no longer there—which would be a heavy blow, since he wouldn't have the first idea how to track her down. That he'd track her down went without saying, if for no other reason than to hear an explanation as to why she'd left.

His concerns were put to rest, however, when Etta emerged from the women's wagon, carrying a basket and heading over to the corral, her graceful skirts swirling around her ankles as she walked.

I bet she can dance, he thought; *dance bare-footed, like those gypsy girls do, even though she's no more a gypsy than I am.* With a mighty effort, he pulled his attention back to finishing-up his meal, and then casually stood, to walk over toward the corral.

Etta had ducked within the roped enclosure, and was —of all things—taking a curry brush to Jenny, and teasing the tangles from her long, curling mane.

Geordie leaned on a tree, and–observing the pile of colorful ribbons in the basket on the ground–drew the obvious conclusion. "So; my Jenny's to be bedecked?"

The lass paused to smile at him over her shoulder. "She is, with your permission, Captain. It is tradition, for the bride to be led to the wedding on her family's finest horse." Her eyes glinting with amusement, she added, "It is not what your Jenny is accustomed to, I imagine."

"Aye; she's a war-horse, born and bred, and she must wonder at it." He realized the words were not necessarily true, though, because the mare stood patiently as Etta began to thread her mane with ribbons, the lass' fingers swift and nimble.

I should move away, Geordie thought reluctantly. *Else Marcello will be over here, quick as a dog guarding a bone.*

As he shifted his weight to turn, however, Etta glanced at him again over her shoulder. "How does your tooth?" she teased.

Ah, he thought; *the lass seeks to keep the conversation going.* Squinting at the sun, Geordie declared, "I've a mind to replace it with a gold one, so's I could look like a pirate. I've always wanted to look like a pirate."

She laughed. "You would only scare the fish."

"The fish fear me, already," he assured her, and she laughed again. *I could listen to that laugh all day long*, he thought in bemusement, *and very soon, I will.*

For a moment, he considered using this opportunity to

ask her about the dead *Rom Baro*—her supposed father—but decided he'd only hear yet another version of events—a fourth version, if he was counting. He shouldn't force the poor lass to make-up a tale for him, especially since she'd been willing to admit that things were not what they seemed. And he'd already gleaned enough to confirm his suspicions that everyone was lying, and that everyone was wary—wary of him, and wary of each other. Except for this lass, who—unless he very much missed his guess—was longing for him almost as much as he was longing for her. It was a heady feeling, and the air between them practically crackled with it.

Therefore, Geordie was unsurprised when Marcello walked over to join them. "We'll go over the plan now, with your permission," the other man offered.

"Willingly," said Geordie, straightening up from his position at the tree. "Teach me to be a Papist priest-although I'm not sure the Padre serves as the best model for me to follow."

"We march with the army we have," Marcello repeated, in a dry tone.

They walked over to where the Padre was seated beneath a shady tree, leaning back, with his flat hat lying on the ground beside him. "Ha," he said, as he watched them approach. "You walk like a soldier, *señor*."

Geordie lowered his large frame to settle in beside the man, and admitted, "There's no help for it; I'll have to pose as one of those Crusaders, rather than some soft priest, who lives a life of wine and ease. Instead, I'll be a warrior-priest, and carry a sword."

"Perhaps not," Marcello suggested with a small smile. "We wish to raise no alarms, after all. Instead, it may be a better strategy if you keep your head lowered, and your steps short. We will keep your part as minimal as possible, but if you are uncertain as to what to do, take any cues from the Padre."

"Aye," Geordie agreed. "And I'm to keep my lip buttoned."

The priest cackled. "If you can manage that, *señor*, it will be a miracle, and I will build a shrine on the very spot."

"I can play-act with the best of them," Geordie protested in a mild tone; "I'm surrounded by experts, after all."

As this comment hung in the air, Marcello offered, "We don't want to expose you as former military, is all. It may arouse suspicions."

Geordie decided he'd not tease the man further, and instead asked, "How long will we be within? Don't Papist weddings go on and on?"

"No—our entire visit should take less than an hour," Marcello replied. "There is no church—not even a chapel —and so there will be an abbreviated ceremony, held in the Comandante's offices."

Geordie nodded. "Is there a retreat route, other than the front gate?"

"There is a second gate at the back, nearer to where we will be," Marcello informed him. "Although it will be guarded, of course."

Geordie squinted up at the branches overhead for a moment. "I'll not go in unarmed."

"No, of course not," Marcello agreed. "But please conceal your weapon carefully. I doubt that we will be searched, but there is always the possibility."

Geordie nodded, somewhat relieved. He'd harbored a fleeting suspicion that he was walking into an ambush—that perhaps the whole point of this elaborate charade was to allow him to be seized by this notorious Rochon fellow. Minos had joked that it was he, who was being hoodwinked, and Geordie would not be at all surprised if this were indeed the case.

But if they were going to let him keep his weapon, this theory seemed unlikely; instead, it made much more sense that the bridegroom wanted Geordie to be present, so as to pass along information about the Colonel. Indeed, it would explain nearly everything that had happened, thus far, including the fairly obvious fact that everyone here wished that he wasn't here—save Etta, of course.

Still and all, he'd best stay sharp. When he'd joked about posing as a warrior-priest, it seemed to him as though Marcello had been a little too quick to turn the subject.

In turn, this reminded him of yet another potential danger, and so when Marcello rose to go over the wedding plan with Gaston and Adao, Geordie leaned back against the tree next to the elderly priest, and shifted his own hat low, so as to cover his face. In a pleasant tone, he said, "I'm convinced this wedding is naught but a sham, Padre. But just in case it isn't, you are not, in truth, to marry the lass to the bridegroom. Just so we are clear."

After a surprised silence, the priest cackled with amusement. "Oh—ho; that's the way of it, then?"

Having taken a good read on his man, Geordie continued, "I will make it worth your while, of course."

"You, *señor*, are my favorite heretic," the priest assured him.

CHAPTER 17

It was late afternoon, and the heat had cooled off, as the wedding party made their way to the gates of the Alcazar. Etta was seated atop Jenny, who was being led by Marcello, with Gaston and Adao flanking him. The Romanies wore their ceremonial clothes, and their movements were accompanied by a pleasant tinkling of the bells that were attached to some of the ribbons, threaded through the mare's mane and tail. The two priests brought up the rear, which gave Geordie a better opportunity to avoid scrutiny, as he kept his head lowered under his flat hat, and covertly surveyed the fort's exterior.

Marcello stepped forward to speak to the guard, and to show him the passage document that had been given them by the Comandante. Whilst they spoke, Geordie allowed his gaze to rest upon the bride for a moment. She was a rare sight, wearing a pretty, loose-sleeved blouse with a colorful sash wound 'round her small waist, her full skirts arrayed over the horse's saddle. The scarf on her head matched the sash, and had ribbons dangling down the back, the same as the ribbons hanging from Jenny's mane and tail. *A bonny lass*, he thought with satisfaction, before he remembered that he should keep his gaze lowered. *So bonny, that I will easily forgive her, if it turns out that she's hoodwinking me, right along with all the others.*

Out of habit, Geordie counted the soldiers in the immediate area, and assessed the best place to make a stand, if a stand were to be needed; it would be a long time before he would shed the habits of war, and he didn't much like walking into a fortified position, where the only escape route would be to battle back through the gate. On the other hand, his mare was a good one for lifting her head and tipping him off, if she sensed trouble, but Jenny was standing placidly, as though having ribbons and bells threaded through her mane and tail was not at all the embarrassment it should be.

"Go in; he's expecting you," the guard advised Marcello, as he returned the passage papers. "I will call for an escort." Their party moved through the gate, but not before Geordie noted with some uneasiness that Adao's face bore a sulky expression that the lad couldn't quite conceal. If Geordie hadn't been playing a priest's part, he'd have cuffed the lad and told him to mind himself; the last needful thing was to draw suspicion.

They proceeded into the graveled yard, where another soldier appeared—a young man who rested an appreciative eye on Etta, before leading the party toward the outbuildings on the far perimeter.

His head lowered and his hands clasped beneath his

cassock, Geordie took a covert survey of the interior courtyard area, as they passed through. It did seem as though there were more guards posted along the walls than would be necessary for this remote outpost; no doubt it was the result of the Frenchman's visit, and the escaped prisoner he'd heard about. He could also sense that the men were being more vigilant than they would normally be—the heightened awareness being the universal language of soldiers who were aware that the brass were unhappy, and they'd best put a good foot forward.

He lowered his gaze again, and plodded along beside the Padre. Bad luck, that security had been tightened, but it shouldn't affect Marcello's plan; there was not much of a defense against Congreve's rockets, which is why all armies, large and small, were scrambling to come up with their own version. Hard on this thought, Geordie glanced over to where the Armory should be, and noted with satisfaction that–although the windowless building had brick walls, as did most armories–the roof was made of wood, and therefore ripe for an overhead attack.

They eventually came to the outbuilding that housed the Comandante's quarters, with one end of it serving as his offices. The commanding officer himself emerged at the guard's knock, looking a bit harassed until he recognized the Spanish priest, and then his expression brightened considerably. "Padre," he said, rubbing his hands together. "Have you brought along anything to celebrate this happy occasion?"

The gleam in the Padre's eyes belied his solemn

expression. "Tomorrow, Comandante. Tomorrow, we will celebrate, as is only fitting."

This seemed a subtle reminder that the fine vintage shouldn't be wasted on the likes of the gypsies, and so the Comandante replied, "*Deo gratias*," and returned a knowing look. He then took a cursory review of the wedding party, and said a bit impatiently, "Bring her inside, then—let's get this over with."

"Your pardon, sir; we cannot come inside—not yet," Marcello explained in a respectful tone. "The horse is part of our ceremony. The bride's tribe presents the girl, along with their best mare as part of her dowry. According to tradition, the bridegroom must first come out and formally indicate he will accept both, before we may enter the building."

The Comandante's mouth twisted in derision, but he duly instructed the guard to fetch the bridegroom from the interior of the building.

Whilst they waited, Geordie caught Etta's eye and winked at her, but she lowered her gaze and made no response. *She's wary,* he thought, *and small blame to her; I should be minding my assignment, instead of trying to tease her.*

The door opened and the guard stepped forward with the bridegroom, who blinked in the late afternoon sun. He was a wiry, swarthy man in the best gypsy tradition, bearing a strong resemblance to Gaston, although he was not as tall. But these things were of little importance in the face of Geordie's extreme surprise, and he had to quickly look down to hide his surge of elation.

For the merciful love of Christ, it was even better

than he could have hoped; the bridegroom was the very same Romany fellow who'd been hanging around Colonel Merryfield. The puzzle pieces immediately fell into place, and it confirmed Geordie's theory; this fellow must have heard that he was looking for information, and he must have insisted that Geordie be included in this wedding party, so as to pass that information along. What an amazing stroke of luck; he'd only to be patient, and give the fellow an opportunity to speak to him privately.

Although Geordie half-expected the bridegroom to meet his eyes in covert acknowledgement, interestingly enough, no such thing happened; instead, the man's gaze was drawn immediately to Etta, seated atop Jenny, and he stepped forward in wonder, as though he'd forgot, for a moment, where he was.

"The *Alkippa*," he breathed.

"The Gypsy Queen, just as we promised," Marcello interjected smoothly. "We hope she meets with your approval."

"Yes; yes, of course." With a visible effort, the man took hold of himself, and formally bowed to Marcello. "I do so approve."

Marcello then stepped forward. "*Pral*," he said formally, and, in a ceremonial manner, kissed Gerard on each cheek.

"*Pral*," Gerard replied.

In turn, Minos and Gaston then stepped forward to formally salute the bridegroom, and Geordie took the opportunity to step forward himself, and greet the man. He didn't speak, but met the other's eyes in silent acknowledgement, only to find that the bridegroom's reaction wasn't at all what he'd expected.

"You!" Gerard hissed, as he drew away from Geordie in astonishment. "What are *you* doing here?"

"Our own priest, from our tribe," Marcello offered into the sudden silence. "As is our tradition."

Geordie was careful to make no response, but he found that he was as astonished as Gerard—this wasn't the reaction he'd been expecting at all, and seemed to turn his theory upside-down; not only was the bridegroom very much surprised to see him, it seemed as though he knew exactly who Geordie was, and was not at all happy to behold him here. *Mayhap the man's smoky, after all*, he thought a bit grimly; *which means I'm due some answers from Marcello.*

"Let's get on with it," said the Comandante, with a touch of impatience.

"Adao," Marcello commanded, with a hint of steel. "You must greet your new brother."

Geordie realized that Adao had not partaken in the greeting ceremony, and in fact, did not seem at all inclined to step forward and bestow the sign of peace upon the bridegroom. Instead he held back, glowering and unhappy, which came as surprise to Geordie—the lad was not one to be sulky.

In a sharp tone, Marcello reprimanded him, "He will be your sister's husband. Do not be a child."

"He does not deserve her—she should not be forced to marry him," the boy lashed out in anger.

"Silence," Marcello commanded, clearly aghast. "You bring shame upon your tribe."

"It is you, who brings shame," the boy returned, furious.

"Adao," said Etta in a pleading tone, as she slid down from Jenny to approach him, her hands held out in a placating gesture. "Brother; please."

But in response, Adao pushed her aside and bore down on the bridegroom, shouting a curse as his hand rose in an arc to bring a dagger down, and drive it into the Romany man's chest.

As Geordie watched in profound disbelief, Gerard clutched at the blade protruding from his chest, and sank down against the door jamb, his expression a mixture of shock and horror. Shouting in outrage, the Romanies moved in as one to converge on Adao, which had the unfortunate effect of blocking Geordie—or the Comandante—from seizing the boy, as he quickly darted out beneath their arms to race over toward Jenny. Shouting the mare into a run, the boy grasped the horse's mane with both hands, bounding along the ground like an acrobat before swinging himself up on her back at a full gallop, the little bells ringing in unison with each powerful stride.

"Stop him!" shouted the Comandante in a furious tone.

Several guards knelt in the dirt to fire upon the fleeing boy, but the sun—low in the sky, in this direction— blinded them from taking an accurate shot.

"Fetch the surgeon!'" shouted the Comandante, as he turned to watch Gaston kneel in horror beside his gasping brother. "And seize that boy!"

"We will, sir—he has nowhere to go," the soldier

shouted in return, but in this, he was mistaken. Before their astonished eyes, Jenny thundered straight toward the back gate and then cleared it with a mighty leap, the shoes on her back hooves flashing briefly in the fading sunlight, before she disappeared from sight.

CHAPTER 18

Into the stunned silence, Etta ran over to Gerard, and began wailing in grief, as she clutched him to her breast. For his part, Geordie stood uncertain, which was a novel experience for him. There was no question that his allegiance was to Etta, but he wasn't certain what he should do, since at present she was hysterically mourning a man she'd never met. She was feigning it, of course; the lass was not a wailer—not by a long shot. He'd best keep his lip buttoned, and hope he could appear as distressed as the others.

"Fetch *Señor* Tello," shouted the Comandante. He stared in horror at Gerard, now lying in a spreading pool of blood, as the other Romanies frantically called to him, and tried to staunch the bleeding. "Ah—*Dios*; don't let him die; quickly, quickly."

In a few moments, a guard approached on the run, accompanied by another man who carried a kit, and appeared to be the surgeon.

"Save him!" the Comandante implored, as the guards

pulled the others away from the fallen man. "*Madre de Dios*, save him—he cannot die!"

Señor Tello knelt down beside Gerard, and carefully removed the knife, pressing down with his hand against the wound as the spreading blood soaked the fallen man's shirt. "It is his heart," the surgeon declared with great regret. "There is nothing to be done."

"*Madre de Dios*," the Comandante repeated in great distress, as he stepped back a pace, closing his eyes. "*Madre de Dios*."

Etta threw her head back, sobbing, as the Padre said gravely, "Let me give him the Sacrament," and surreptitiously squeezed Geordie's arm as he passed by.

Thus reminded, Geordie knelt alongside the Padre, and copied his movements, whilst Etta sobbed in anguish, and the assembled Romanies solemnly removed their hats. Geordie wasn't fooled, though; he'd seen many a dying man, and–although Gerard was awash in blood– he did not have the waxen look of a man who was sinking into himself.

Whilst the Comandante alternatively cursed and shouted orders to pursue Adao, the Padre concluded the rite, lifting a hand to gently close Gerard's eyelids. He and Geordie then rose, whilst Gaston took off his coat, and lay it reverently over the supposedly dead man.

"We will take him," Marcello offered. "He must be buried with our rituals."

"Out of my sight! Out of my sight–all of you!" the Comandante ground out in a fury. "And curse every gypsy who ever lived!" He directed the waiting soldiers,

"Bring me that boy—send another search party; quickly, it is fast turning dark."

Whilst the remaining soldiers scrambled to do his bidding, a young woman pushed a garden barrow over toward them, and the gypsies carefully loaded the bundled-up corpse into her cart.

As no one had called for this assistance, Geordie surmised that this was the kitchen girl who was an ally, and so he lingered within earshot, and was unsurprised when Marcello asked her in a low voice, "When will he return?"

"Tomorrow, mid-day," the girl murmured, without looking at him.

"Many thanks," Marcello replied.

They speak of the Frenchman, Geordie guessed. *This Frenchman does not sound like someone who'd be as easily fooled as the Comandante, and so he's been called away, on a contrivance. Which means that this extraction has all the earmarks of a carefully-managed operation, but damned if that doesn't leave me with more questions than answers.*

With Etta wringing her hands and weeping, the gypsies made a solemn procession toward the front gate. Geordie copied the Padre's mournful pose, as they walked together, even though he was on high-alert, and wished they could proceed a bit faster toward safety. To the good, most of the soldiers had dashed off in pursuit of Adao, which meant that there were fewer posted along their route. Although their little party was the subject of open curiosity, no one interrupted their sad journey, with the occasional soldier making the Sign of the Cross, as they passed by.

Geordie quickened his pace, so that he wound up walking abreast with Marcello, and—with a bent head—he murmured, "I suppose there is no chance they will catch the lad?"

"None," Marcello replied.

Geordie continued in an ominous tone, "You've lied to me again, you gingin' bogger, and you'd have thought you'd learned your lesson, by now. If it weren't for Etta, I'd make you pay for it, and sorely."

"I am truly sorry, Captain," the man replied in a quiet tone. "But you would find the truth more unbelievable than the lie."

CHAPTER 19

I'll have my horse back, or know the reason why, Geordie thought grimly. In truth, it was the most fantastic thing out of all the fantastic things that had happened, this day; Jenny had abandoned him without a second's hesitation. It was very unlike her, and was–truth to tell—a bit unsettling. They did say that the gypsies had a way with horses, but he'd been shocked to the core, that the mare had so willingly left him behind.

As night fell, the Romany campsite had been quietly packed up, with the two caravan wagons lumbering down the nearest road toward the west. This was not a surprise to Geordie, since it was apparent that this rescue operation was well thought-out, and it would behoove the participants to be gone without a trace when the Frenchman came back the next day, and discovered that his valuable prisoner had been murdered.

And with this in mind, Geordie was also unsurprised to see several shadowy figures emerge from a copse of trees along the road—men who swung themselves up into the caravans, and took-up the reins without a word, whilst the gypsies—and Geordie—exchanged places with them, and slipped away into the trees. The wagons would lay a false trail away from here, but the rescuers would remain behind. This operation was not yet complete, after all; there was a rocket attack in the works, now that the valuable prisoner had been removed from the fort.

Geordie held his tongue throughout these developments, and noted that when they arrived at what appeared to be their object—a large house in Santa Luisa—the two Brittany brothers, Gerard and Gaston, parted from the group to go into the house, along with Marcello and Etta. The rest of them were left to slip quietly into the stables, where they were greeted by the same girl who'd been an ally within the walls—Ines, her name was. The Padre then left to return to his own home, and no one spoke a word, as Ines whispered that there was bread and cheese, along with blankets, hidden in the loft.

It was a strange feeling, to have to possess his soul in patience. If Geordie had been left to his own devices, he'd have promptly used his fists to get some answers, but until he discovered how Etta fit in, he restrained himself. She'd played the widowed bride so well, he wondered if perhaps she was an actress, hired to play the part. It didn't make much sense to him, though; the actresses he'd known—and he'd known a few—tended to be cut from a different cloth than Etta, with her reserved manner, and winsome ways. In truth, he'd never have believed it of her, had he not seen it with his own eyes; it didn't shake his complete certainty that they were meant for each other, but it did raise some very disquieting questions.

In the end, he figured that he'd three objectives; first, he'd go wherever Etta went, second, he'd get his damned horse back, and third—by God—he'd find out what Gerard-the-dead-bridegroom knew about Colonel Merryfield's death. It was a shame that his original theory had been proved wrong, but it seemed clear the man knew *something*, or he wouldn't have reacted with such dismay, when he'd come face-to-face with Geordie.

The group climbed into the stable loft to eat the bread and cheese, staying quiet as they ate the cold meal, and drank out of water flasks. When Gaston and Marcello slipped through the stable door to climb the ladder and join them, however, Geordie found he could no longer contain himself, and said in a low voice, "It was a beltin' good rescue, I'll give you that; but I don't understand why I was duped to come along. I was as useless as tits on a boar."

Minos smiled at this characterization, but Gaston reached for more cheese, and replied in a terse tone, "We could not trust you with the plan, *gadjo*. You are English."

"Scottish," Geordie corrected patiently. "Not the same at all. And if you couldn't trust me, then why rope me into this charade, in the first place?"

It seemed to Geordie there was a heavy silence, as the men kept their heads down, and continued to eat. Minos was the one who broke it, when he replied with a shrug, "You are here, *gadjo*, because the *Alkippa*—the Gypsy Queen—insisted that you be."

Quickly, Geordie decided he'd best change the subject,

what with Marcello sitting there—best let the man realize in a more gradual fashion that he was slated to lose his pretty kinswoman to a rough Scotsman. Fortunately, there was another subject that Geordie could raise, and so he addressed Marcello bluntly, "I'll ask again; are you working for the British?"

"No," Marcello replied, as he took another bite of the bread.

Geordie wasn't certain whether he believed him; he was somewhat familiar with the British spymaster, having been recruited by the man. Geordie had declined the invitation, being as it was not in his nature to skulk about and feign things—his recent role as a Papist priest —for the merciful love of Christ—ably demonstrating this fact. But this was a well-planned-out rescue scheme, and he was almost certain that the fine hand of the spymaster was behind it. It would be surprising if this was not the case, in fact, despite whatever tale Marcello was trying to feed him.

"I'd like some answers," said Geordie in no uncertain terms. "And I'll have my horse back."

"She's not your horse, *gadjo*." Adao's voice, laden with humor, floated up to him from below.

Astonished, Geordie scrambled to the edge of the loft, and then leapt down the ladder, so as to stride over to the far stall. There he beheld the welcome sight of Jenny, standing placidly as she munched on oats from a halter-feed.

"Lass," he breathed in mock-annoyance, as he carefully ran his hands down her front legs. "I should feed you to the crows, for giving me such a turn."

He straightened up to cuff Adao on the back of his head. "And you along with her, laddie."

Adao only grinned in response, and Geordie couldn't begrudge the lad; it was a heady feeling, to have outfoxed the enemy, and he'd let the boy revel in it.

Geordie looked over at the others, who were now filing into the stall behind him. "Shouldn't we hide her? She's fair recognizable, and even more so, now."

"We have sentries posted," Marcello explained. "We will have warning, if there is a search, and we can always lead her into the smokehouse, if necessary."

Geordie nodded. "And Gerard? He's hid away too?" Mainly, Geordie was in a fever to have a private conversation with the man.

"He will stay within the house, posing as a guest," Marcello replied. "There is a hidden room where he can withdraw, if a search is mounted."

Again, Geordie nodded, and came to grips with the realization that he was not in the chain of command for this operation, which was a very strange and disconcerting feeling. Nevertheless, he could demand some answers, and sooner rather than later. "I'll hear your tale, then, with no bark on it. I'm not someone who likes being led on a may-dance, and my patience is worn thin. Why was I enlisted in this operation?"

There was a small silence, and Geordie observed the interesting fact that Marcello glanced at Minos, as though seeking direction. This was not much of a surprise to Geordie; he'd already come to the conclusion that the clownish little man wasn't such a clown, after all.

"Fah; you may as well tell him," Mino declared, spreading his hands. "He'll not believe it, anyways."

CHAPTER 20

Geordie huddled with the other men, seated on the stall's floor, so as to keep their voices from carrying. "Let's start at the beginning, then," he began quietly. "Why was I recruited for this plot? Why go to the trouble, with poor Angus bribed to feed me a false tale?"

Minos sighed, and shrugged his shoulders. "We didn't recruit you, *gadjo*; the *Alkippa* recruited you. She is the Gypsy Queen, and her wishes cannot be ignored."

Geordie raised his brows in bewilderment. "*Etta* recruited me?"

"I am afraid you are laboring under a misapprehension, Captain," Marcello offered. "Etta is not the *Alkippa*; your horse is the *Alkippa*."

"My horse? Jenny?" Geordie glanced over at his mare, who was standing half-asleep, and then stared at the circle of intent faces that surrounded him. "I don't understand."

"The black mare is the Gypsy Queen," Marcello

explained, with a nod toward the horse. "The gypsy tribes do not have kings or queens, as such. But the *Alkippa* is their legendary Queen." It was clear that Marcello was carefully choosing his words, so as to not give offense. "She is rather like a totem, and is believed to have mystical powers."

Geordie looked at the other men's faces, and saw that they were completely serious. Smiling, he drew a hand down over his face. "My Jenny's magic, you're saying? Pull the other one, lads."

"She was my father's horse," Adao insisted. "He knew."

But Geordie only shook his head—not unkindly, since the boy was young, and wanted to revere his father, as was right. "That's unlikely, lad; Jenny's not old enough to have been your father's horse—not unless she was but a foal, at the time. And aside from that, she's a trained war horse, and belonged to a soldier who fell at Badajoz."

"Perhaps, perhaps not," said Minos, with a tilt of his head. "But Adao is an excellent stealer-of-horses, and the *Alkippa* would not stay stolen. She insisted that you come along."

The light dawned, and Geordie had to chuckle aloud. "So; it was you lot, then, who kept stealing my Jenny? It serves you right; the lass is an escape artist, and can jump a fence like no other." He ran an amused glance around the group, but saw that they remained in deadly earnest, and it suddenly occurred to him that they wouldn't have planned this scheme, unless they were confident they'd a horse who could clear a six-foot gate with Adao on her back—no easy feat for any horse.

A bit unsettled by this realization, he asked, "How did you know that I had her in the first place?"

Gaston spoke up from the shadows. "My brother, Gerard. He spent some time at the British Army camp, and he sent a message to me, to tell me—with much amazement–that one of the English soldiers rode the *Alkippa*, all unknowing."

"We were all amazed to hear it," Minos confirmed. "But her choices cannot be questioned."

"More like I chose her, friends," Geordie explained, a bit bemused. "She was running loose on the battlefield."

"You are not a *Rom*," Minos offered fairly, "and so you cannot be blamed for thinking such a thing."

Geordie blew out a breath, having decided that mayhap he should not discourage this idea that the horse was bound to him, in some way, since it meant he would be allowed to walk away with her, once this little adventure came to an end. Although he'd also have a wife who would be worth any number of magic horses, if it came to that. Hopefully, he'd manage to walk away with both.

Thinking of this, he asked, "So; what's to happen, now? Was the payment you promised me just a tale, to bring me along with my horse?"

"Oh, no," said Marcello immediately. "You will be paid as promised. And we hope you will indeed help us launch a rocket attack, as soon as possible."

"You are going after Rochon, the Frenchman," Geordie guessed. "Who will return tomorrow."

"We are going after the Alcazar," Marcello corrected.

"But we would not grieve for the Frenchman, if he were to fall."

Again, Geordie drew a hand down over his face. "I'll be the first to admit that I'm in over my head," he declared. "And with this in mind, I am reluctant to trust any of you a farthing's worth, especially after being roundly hoodwinked, with nearly every step I take."

"I can give you assurances," Marcello offered.

Geordie considered this; he wasn't necessarily inclined to trust anything Marcello told him—not after the trick he'd pulled today—but on the other hand, he'd little choice, if he was going to emerge from this briar-patch with bonny Etta by his side. "Let's hear them, then," he replied.

"Come; we will take a walk," Marcello said, and then he rose to head toward the stable door.

CHAPTER 21

Geordie accompanied Marcello out the wide wooden door, and thought it interesting that the other man seemed to have no fear of walking forth from their hiding place. He'd mentioned that there were people posted to give warning, if anyone approached, but Geordie had known more than a few sentries who'd fallen short, in that department, and so he tended to trust only his own assessment.

Therefore, as they stepped out into a graveled yard that stretched between the stables and the main house, Geordie paused to listen, and carefully survey the shadows. The yard was ringed by old-growth trees, and a small, brick building stood about half-way between the house and the stables—it must be the smokehouse, that Marcello had mentioned. A lighted lamp shone from one of the kitchen windows in the main house, and all seemed quiet.

Marcello suggested, "Perhaps we should take a turn around the perimeter."

"You've a fair amount of trust, in your sentries," Geordie noted.

"Yes," Marcello agreed. "With good reason."

"Well, I don't trust any single one of you," Geordie continued, as the two men began to walk toward the tree line. "What in the name of Christ is going on, here?"

"It is as Minos said," Marcello explained, as they paused in the shadow of the trees, and looked back upon the deserted yard, illuminated by the single lamp. "The horse is the *Alkippa,* and it seems that the horse insisted that you be included in the rescue operation."

Geordie glanced over at him. "But you don't believe that nonsense—not for a minute."

Marcello hesitated, and so Geordie cut to the nub. "You're no more a gypsy than I am, friend. I'd like to hear why I'm being led on a may-game, with the story changing nearly every hour."

The other man bowed his head, so as to contemplate the ground, and chose his words carefully. "I am not a Romany, it is true. But I would rather not tell you which interests I do serve."

"Everyone here has different interests," Geordie agreed. "But you are all allied in this operation, for some reason—some more reluctant than others, I think."

"Yes," his companion agreed, and offered nothing more.

Geordie eyed him. "Do the British know that you mean to destroy the Alcazar?"

The question hung in the air for a moment, and then Marcello replied carefully, "Not officially."

Geordie nodded, as he'd drawn this conclusion on his own. The British couldn't openly move to destroy a Spanish fort—not with the peace negotiations hanging in the balance—but it seemed unlikely that Marcello would make such a bold attempt without their knowledge, and their connivance. The British held the whip-hand, in Spain, after all, and repercussions would be swift and terrible, if this rag-tag group of gypsies gainsaid the wishes of the British Army; therefore, the British Army must be backing them—although not overtly, of course. Indeed, it would explain the precision of the plan, and Geordie's sure sense that the British spymaster must be involved, somehow. It would also explain why Geordie had been recruited to help, instead of the official British rocketeers. The official rocketeers would be harder to explain away, if they were caught.

Geordie tilted his head. "Yet you keep telling me you aren't a British spy."

"No. As you said, the group has diverse motives." His companion paused for a moment, as though weighing what to say, and then admitted, "My own motive is vengeance."

Surprised, Geordie stared at him for a moment, and then chuckled. "Now; there's *finally* something I can understand. Who's being avenged?"

"One of my kinsmen was sore-wounded at Rochon's hands, recently. Such a thing will not go unpunished."

"Absolutely," Geordie agreed. "Between you and these Romanies, it's bloody vengeance atop bloody vengeance, and you're lucky you've a Scotsman, to show you how it's done." Not to mention there would be no better way to curry favor with his future in-laws—one would think—than to wipe-out their enemies.

Marcello unbent enough to smile slightly. "Indeed. We will have additional men in the morning, with one being a blacksmith."

Geordie nodded his approval. "Have you black powder? You'll need a fair amount."

"Yes—it is already stored in this very smokehouse."

Thinking it over Geordie added, "We'll need to fetch the Padre, in the morning—here's hoping he'll not be suffering from the drink, and has a clear head."

A bit alarmed, Marcello glanced at him. "Why do you seek out the Padre?"

Geordie smiled. "He's slated to deliver wine to the Comandante tomorrow. It's a godsend; we'll put him to use."

"If you say," Marcello offered in a doubtful tone.

"You'll see." Geordie then caught himself, as he realized that he was busy charting-out the attack, when he hadn't been given any assurances at all—only Marcello's oblique admission that the British were involved, and that admission might well be lies upon more lies. But he didn't think the man was lying—in fact, he'd the sure sense that he was finally glimpsing a bit of the truth, at long last.

Marcello's voice broke into his thoughts. "Out of curiosity, Captain, I would like to ask you–just between us. Your mare–"

"My magic mare," Geordie offered with a smile, having a good guess as to the next question.

Marcello offered his own slightly sheepish smile in

response. "Yes. I'll admit that I am intrigued. Had you any hint that she was—that she is revered by the Romanies?"

"She's a doughty lass," Geordie declared. "But she's just a horse, friend. Never say you buy into this nonsense?" This would be a surprise; he'd the strong impression that Marcello was a hard-headed man, and didn't believe that the horse was magic any more than Geordie did.

Again, Marcello smiled slightly. "No—of course not. But I did wonder why Gerard seemed so unhappy to see you, at the wedding. I thought perhaps it had to do with the mare."

Since Geordie had wondered about Gerard's reaction himself, he offered his own conclusion. "I've never met the man, but I've seen him at the British camp, in the company of my commanding officer." He paused, and decided he may as well be honest, even if it seemed that he was the only one, in this God-forsaken group. "I wondered whether he might be involved in my commanding officer's murder."

Gravely, Marcello cautioned, "Even if that is the case, Captain, you mustn't kill Gerard. This would be a situation where vengeance should be forsworn, for the greater good."

"I'll make my own assessment on the subject, if you don't mind," Geordie replied, barely keeping his temper in check. "I'm mighty tired of being lied to."

With mock-politeness, he then tugged on the brim of his hat, but before he turned to leave, Marcello stayed him with a hand. "Hold, Captain; Etta has asked for leave to speak to you. A half-hour, in the house." He glanced up, in the direction of the light in the window.

This was a welcome surprise, but Geordie could sense the man's disquiet, hidden beneath his reserve, and so he said with all sincerity, "I'd never disrespect the lass; you've my oath on it."

"A half-hour," Marcello repeated, and then he turned to silently retreat back into the stables.

*B*efore going in to the house, Geordie paused at the pump to wash his face and hands—he didn't want the lass to think he was uncivilized, after all—and whilst he smoothed his hair back with wet hands, he contemplated the interesting fact that—although the Padre seemed convinced that Marcello's objective was the mysterious treasure-casket—Marcello himself had still made no mention of it, even when he'd finally shone a sliver of honesty on this twisting tale. *No one should be trusted*, Geordie reminded himself. *Watch yourself, laddie.*

He tapped softly on the kitchen door, which was promptly opened by Ines, who appeared to have been waiting to let him in. She was a pretty lass, about Etta's age, and wore her dark hair loose so that the ends curled nicely along her cleavage—not that any more attention needed to be drawn; the lass had an impressive stretch of cleavage, truth be told.

"Follow me," she whispered, but not before she'd boldly met his eyes, an invitation contained in her own.

He was careful not to respond to it, as he returned a respectful greeting. A minx, she was, and a bit too practiced, for his taste. Not to mention he was courting, and therefore shouldn't be distracted by buxom minxes.

Ines led him down a hallway and into the dining room, the room illuminated by an oil lamp, on the table. Etta sat in one of the chairs, awaiting him, and the lass looked up upon his entrance. She was no longer wearing her gypsy garb, but instead was dressed in a demure frock, appropriate for a Spanish girl her age, with her hair braided atop her head. All in all, he rather preferred the gypsy garb, but he understood the need for disguise. The curves of her face were illuminated in the glow of the lamp, and as her eyes met his, he caught his breath for a moment. *Here's a sight*, he thought; *and here's where I belong, at long last.*

"Lass," he greeted her respectfully, holding his hat in his hands. From the corner of his eye, he could see a figure sitting in the adjacent drawing room–an elderly woman, dressed in black, and sitting stick-straight in a chair, as she read a book. They were to be chaperoned, then—as was only was to be expected. To the good, however, if they spoke in low voices, no one would be able to overhear.

Because time was short, as Geordie settled into a chair, he asked, "Is Etta your true name?"

She nodded. "Margaretta," she replied, and a small dimple played around her cheek.

Lord, she was comely, but he had to focus, and stay on-task. "How do I find you, if we are parted?" This was a serious concern, in the event the various deceivers that surrounded him all decided to melt away. He would have no idea where to start.

The clear green eyes met his for a moment, and the expression in them turned regretful. "I am afraid I cannot say, Captain. I am sorry—and I also wanted to say I am sorry I could not tell you what was planned, today."

"Dinna apologize, lass, I understand." He didn't have the heart to press her for any more information that she probably wasn't allowed to give him, and so he changed the subject. "Margaretta's a bonnie name—there's a Saint Margaret, in Scotland's history; she's very famous."

Etta leaned forward; her interest caught. "Have you saints, in Scotland? I didn't think you did."

"Of course, we do," he declared. "Not like the Papists, though—none of that foolishness with candles, and statues, and such."

She made no response, only sat unmoving, and in turn, he paused, thoroughly aghast. "Never say you're a Papist?"

Slowly, she nodded. "I am afraid so, Captain."

With a mighty effort, Geordie tempered his reaction, and assured her, "You can be whatever you wish, lassie; I've no objection." Mentally, he quickly quashed an image of his grandfather, who'd fought at Culloden, rolling over in his grave. "I wish you'd tell me where you hail from, though; if I'm to live there, I should know."

But she raised her brows in surprise. "I thought we were going to fish in the River Tween."

Very pleased that she'd remembered, he explained, "'Tis 'Tweed', lass. And it's fine fishing, but Scotland's cold, when all is said and done, and I don't think you're one who's much-used to cold weather. I'll be happy to abide where you abide." This was actually true; Geordie was not the sort to be home-bound, which was why he'd signed up for the Army at his first opportunity.

She offered doubtfully, "My home is quite hot, much of the time. I am not certain you would tolerate it very well."

He smiled, touched that she was worried about him. "We're like chalk and cheese, then."

"Yes." The dimple appeared again, because apparently this was no more a concern to her than it was to him, and it engendered within his breast a yearning that was so powerful he was nearly bowled over by the strength of it. They'd live their days together, he was certain of it; he'd find a way, and with this in mind, he'd best get down to brass tacks.

Lowering his voice still further, he began, "I swear I won't repeat anything you say, lass, or let on that you've told me, but I need to see if this story hangs together."

She nodded in understanding. "I will tell you what I can, Captain."

"Geordie," he corrected.

She smiled again. "Geordie," she repeated softly, and he resisted a mighty urge to kiss her soft mouth, then and there.

Instead, he asked, "What is Marcello to you?"

Without hesitation, she replied, "He is my brother."

"And you've a kinsman, who was wounded?"

Her brow clouded slightly with the memory. "Yes. Catalo."

This was almost a surprise, because Geordie had

halfway convinced himself that Marcello's vengeance story was yet another false tale—Marcello didn't seem the avenging type. "Is your kinsman being held in the Alcazar?" This would serve as a complication, if they were going to burn the place down.

"No, he is safe. He is in–" she paused, and he could see that she caught herself, because apparently to say where the man was, would be to give something away.

Geordie let it go, since as long as it wasn't another hurdle in his plans, he didn't much care. Instead, he said firmly, "Lass, I know I don't have the ordering of you—not yet, leastways–but I don't know what your brother was thinking, to pull you into harm's way like he has–"

He stopped suddenly, seeing the expression in her eyes, as she regarded him in silent astonishment. There was a long pause, whilst—with a mighty effort—Geordie readjusted his entire way of thinking. "I'm that sorry," he offered humbly. "Can you pretend I didn't say it?"

"You are kind to be concerned," she said gently. "But I am not one of your soldiers."

Unable to resist, he took her hand, and bent his head as he fingered it in his own. "I'm that sorry," he repeated. "And shame on me–I've known my share of doughty lasses, and you're as doughty as they come. But I can't be easy, with the way you risked yourself."

"You must never say such a thing again," she teased, bending her head so as to look into his face with a small smile.

"I don't know as I can promise," he admitted. "But you're always to speak freely to me, lass, and I'll always listen. My oath on it."

In the next room, the elderly woman made a show of closing her book, and hurriedly, Etta leaned in and whispered, "Before you go, I must tell you two things."

"Let's hear it," he said quietly, keeping his gaze on her hands, clasped in his.

Her head bent close, she continued, "I overheard Gerard, speaking to Gaston. He seemed angry."

This was of interest, and Geordie said slowly, "Now, there's a corker. You'd think he'd be falling on his brother's neck, and weeping in gratitude."

Quickly, Etta glanced sidelong toward their chaperone, and continued, "They spoke of you. Gerard called you 'the surety', and was very unhappy you were here; he wanted to blame Gaston, but Gaston said he was given no choice."

With a knit brow, Geordie admitted, "I've no clue what that's about, lass. What was the second thing?"

She hesitated, and then revealed with some concern, "Ines thinks you are handsome."

Very much enjoying this glimpse of jealousy, Geordie feigned astonishment. "Does she? Does she know I lack a tooth?"

But Etta would not be teased, and warned in all seriousness, "I think she means to seduce you."

"I thank you for the warning," Geordie said gravely. "She'll not succeed."

Their chaperone could be seen to rise to her feet, and so in turn, Geordie rose to take his leave. "Good night, lass," he said, and bowed formally.

"The Padre would know how to find me," Etta whispered hurriedly, as she curtseyed in return.

ased on the alarming bit of news he'd heard from Etta, Geordie decided that he should try to stall his departure from the house, and hope to hear a bit more about why the two Romany brothers were arguing about him. He hadn't wanted to alarm Etta, but the words she'd heard made it sound as though some sort of trap had been set up for him. It appeared that the trap was not here in Santa Luisa—since Gerard was not at all happy to see him here—but the words they'd used left Geordie with the uneasy conviction that the people who'd come after the Colonel were now coming after him, and therefore it would behoove him to find out more about it.

To this end, he paused in the kitchen, and asked Ines, "Is there any cornbread about, lass? I confess I'm sharp-set."

"There is almond cake," she offered, and she crossed over to the pantry, brushing up against him as she did so. "I will be happy to slice you a piece." She threw him a meaningful glance over her shoulder.

Now, there's an invitation if I ever saw one, he thought, and wondered how he could manage to tarry here in the kitchen without Etta's hearing about it, and drawing all the wrong conclusions. Fortunately, he wasn't called upon to defend his virtue, because–just as he'd half-hoped–the figure of Gerard appeared in the doorway, holding a candle and looking mighty harassed.

"A good evening to you," Geordie offered in a genial tone. "I'm having a bite o' cake, friend—won't you join me?"

But the Romany man only waved Ines away, and tugged on Geordie's elbow with some urgency, so as to draw him over toward the wall. "What are *you* doing here?" he hissed furiously. "Why aren't you in Sheffield?"

This was unexpected, and Geordie raised his brows. "Why would I go to Sheffield?"

"The mortgage," the Romany man whispered in an urgent tone. "What has happened to the mortgage?"

Geordie gazed at him, wide-eyed, and shook his head. "I don't know what you're talking about, friend."

"The *mortgage*, you fool," the other man ground out in exasperation. "I'm the one who drew it up."

With a great deal of force, Geordie grasped the smaller man by his jacket shoulders, and slammed him up against the wall, pinning him there with a forearm to his abdomen, and leaning in with a great deal of menace. "Tell me," he said in a deceptively soft tone, "what you know of Colonel Merryfield's death."

"Ah—ah, *gadjo*," the man gasped; "you mistake—you mistake."

They were interrupted when a voice called out from

the doorway, "Excuse me, *señores*; but there is to be no brawling in the house." The elderly woman stood beside Ines, her face solemn in the flickering candlelight.

"I beg your pardon, ma'am," Geordie said, as he let Gerard fall to the floor with a thud. "We'll take it outside."

"I believe this gentleman is not to go out-of-doors, *señor*."

"Then I will take my leave, ma'am," said Geordie, who lifted his hat in an ironic gesture, and then turned to depart with no further ado.

Once outside on the kitchen stoop, Geordie took a long breath of the night air, as he paused to take a careful survey of the yard. He'd wait a moment before going back to the stables—he needed to cool his temper, and clear his head, and think about what he'd just learned, since it seemed mighty significant.

Somehow, Colonel Merryfield's silver mines were involved, and—now that he thought about it—he was a right nodcock, not to have considered this aspect, before. If there was a fortune at stake, everyone's motivations would suddenly start to make a lot more sense—not to mention it would also explain the true reason for Geordie's own inclusion in this plot, since his supposedly magic horse was the thinnest of excuses.

Gerard said he was the one who'd drawn up a mortgage on the Colonel's mines—fake, perhaps, since the man was a counterfeiter, by trade? And the Colonel had then handed over that mortgage to Geordie, all quiet-like, just before he'd died, and at the same time had strongly hinted that Geordie should marry his daughter.

And now that same counterfeiter wondered—with grave alarm—why Geordie hadn't gone off to Sheffield, presumably to lay claim to the silver mines.

The more he thought about it, the less it looked as though Gerard was a bad 'un, and so mayhap he didn't deserve the rough treatment that Geordie had just meted out. Obviously, the Colonel and Gerard had been working together on this secret mortgage business, and Geordie knew with complete certainty that the Colonel was not going to send him into a trap—especially if he were wed to the man's daughter.

And there was the interesting fact that Gerard had referred to Geordie as the 'surety,' when he didn't know that he was being overheard. And finally, there was the undeniable fact that Gerard had seemed genuinely unhappy to behold him here in Spain, in the thick of whatever was going on.

Therefore, it did seem as though Geordie was to act as some sort of back-up to whatever the Colonel's plan was —that's what a 'surety' was, after all. That there'd been a plan seemed evident; before he'd been killed, the Colonel had the look of a man who knew that any moment might be his last—not to mention that he was trying to secure his daughter's future, even though she wasn't yet of age. But Geordie had thwarted the plan, by stubbornly staying in Spain so as to seek justice for the man, rather than go lay claim to—for the merciful love of Christ–silver mines in Sheffield.

And so, it did seem—based on events—that Geordie could tentatively conclude that Gerard was not, in fact, a scoundrel. Neither was Gaston, for that matter, since both brothers knew that Geordie was acting as the surety, to stop whatever the enemy had planned—a counterfeiting operation, it seemed. No point in Napoleon's plotting a counterfeiting operation, if the silver mines were under the control of a former British soldier. The Colonel had concocted a plan to thwart the enemy's operation, and then reward Geordie with a bride and a fortune, all in one fell swoop.

It was a shame, almost, that he was such a stubborn boyo, and had stayed behind to see that the Colonel's good name was cleared. *I threw a spanner in the works, and didn't do what I was supposed to,* Geordie thought with some regret; *I hope that his poor daughter has managed to survive without me.*

With this revelation in mind, it was tempting to take hold of Etta and clear out with all speed, to go lay claim to the mines. He wouldn't, though—not yet; because there was something here that he didn't understand. Etta and Marcello weren't gypsies, and it seemed obvious that they weren't any part of the plan cooked-up betwixt Gerard and the Colonel, since Etta had eavesdropped on the gypsy brothers' conversation, and had then reported it back to him. This would align with his sense that Etta and her brother weren't allied with anyone else—they were here on their own mission, separate and apart from the others—vengeance, supposedly, for their wounded kinsman. Not to mention they were from someplace hot— probably somewhere in the Mediterranean, from the looks of them.

Although, come to think of it, the lass had said the Padre would know how to find her. Why would the local

Padre have any such knowledge, if the lass wasn't from around these parts? They were all Papists, of course, which may be what she'd meant; presumably the Padre could ask along his network of priests, or some such.

"Excuse me," a voice spoke from the smokehouse shadows. "Do you mind if I smoke?"

With a quick movement, Geordie's pistol was in his hand—confound it, he was getting soft, if he hadn't realized the man was there. To the good, the fellow didn't seem to be a danger, since he'd passed on the opportunity to shoot at Geordie from the shadows. "Show yourself, friend."

"I'd rather not. We have met before, though." With a flare of flame, the man lit his pipe, and in the light of the lucifer, Geordie saw the other's face, and recognized a familiar pair of grey eyes. It was the British spymaster, who'd once tried to recruit him into the spying business.

"Sir," Geordie said, as he sheathed his pistol, and walked over to join the man in the shadows. *Lord alive*, he thought with resignation; *I'll be more than ready for my bed, when everyone's had their say.*

CHAPTER 24

The grey-eyed man drew on the pipe for a moment. "I understand you are reluctant to proceed, absent assurances."

So; Marcello was obviously in contact with this man—although Marcello had disavowed being a British spy. Which could have been a lie, after all; everyone around him lied as easily as they drew breath. Except his bonny Etta, of course—although mayhap he shouldn't be too sure about that, either.

Geordie nodded. "Aye; I wouldn't want to undermine British interests."

The grey eyes flicked toward his. "You wouldn't be."

Geordie nodded, aware that—for obvious reasons—the British couldn't openly support the take-down of a Spanish fort in peace time. "What are the rules of engagement?"

"The rules of engagement are whatever you wish them to be."

Geordie noted, "Marcello doesn't want a lot of casualties, which is probably wise."

The spymaster nodded. "His assistance in this matter is much-appreciated, and so I would bow to his wishes."

Geordie decided he may as well say, "On the other hand, it seems that few would grieve for the Frenchman, were he to fall."

There was a small silence, and then his companion noted, "You are very well-informed, Captain."

"Not necessarily," Geordie replied, and let the words hang in the air.

The other man removed his pipe, and contemplated the distance for a moment. "It is peace-time, Captain, and *Monsieur* Rochon is an important man. My hands are tied, and I cannot move against him. The enemy would show the same restraint, if it were me."

That's interesting, thought Geordie; *apparently, the spymaster's not aware that Marcello has his own vengeance-plans. Lord, everyone has cross-purposes, and it's making my head ache, trying to sort them all out.*

Thinking about his own purposes, he decided to test-out what the spymaster knew about Gerard's plan with the Colonel. "Can you trust Gerard to help you, now that he's been rescued? What are his allegiances?"

The man's mouth twisted. "At present, Gerard will pledge allegiance to anyone who doesn't threaten his life."

But Geordie had to tilt his head in mild disagreement. "He's too valuable to be killed by either side, I reckon."

The spymaster regarded him for a moment, his face illuminated by the glowing embers in his pipe bowl. "A good point. More correctly, it is a matter of keeping him from being valuable to the enemy."

Geordie nodded at this veiled reference to the enemy's counterfeiting operation, and decided that he may as well openly broach the subject, and see what the other man had to say. "I'd seen Gerard before—at the camp, and hanging about with Colonel Merryfield, of all people. Did he have anything to do with the Colonel's death?"

The grey eyes glinted up to his, briefly. "No. I am afraid only Colonel Merryfield can be held responsible for his death."

There was an edge of censure to his tone, but Geordie only nodded, and lowered his gaze so as to tamp down his inclination to leap to the Colonel's defense. *So*, he thought; *the spymaster doesn't know about the mortgage, it seems, and he doesn't know that Gerard was the Colonel's ally.*

And this seemed rather strange, but until he knew more, he should probably continue to keep his lip buttoned—there was something here that he didn't understand, and it raised the point that seemed to be the crux of this puzzle; the Colonel and Gerard had concocted a back-up plan, with a false mortgage in Geordie's name so that he could claim the mines in Sheffield—presumably in the event the Colonel was killed. But why go to such lengths? If the enemy wanted to lay hands on the silver mines, why not simply inform the spymaster of this—he was clearly a very capable fellow, and well-able to thwart such a plot. The only conclusion that Geordie could reach—and it made him very uneasy—was that the Colonel didn't want the spymaster—or anyone—to know what he and Gerard were planning.

Geordie did not believe for a moment that the Colonel would betray the British—not for a single moment—but surely, the Colonel could trust the spymaster? So why did it seem as though the Colonel felt he had to work alone, to create his own fail-safe? And why would Gerard still be keeping the Colonel's secrets, even after the man had been killed?

Thinking it best not to voice these thoughts aloud, Geordie instead remarked, "Lucky to be Gerard; each side's trying to out-bribe the other."

With a sigh, his companion lowered his pipe to tap the ashes from it, against the stone wall. "Yes; we were fortunate to discover that Gerard has a fancy to become the next King of the Gypsies. There is a dearth in leadership, at present, and it is his fond wish to unite the tribes that remain, with himself at their head. The British have agreed to aid him in this endeavor, in return for his allegiance." The man glanced up at Geordie. "To this end, he was promised the Gypsy Queen."

Geordie stared at him in frank disbelief. "My horse? You can't believe this wild tale they tell about her, surely?"

"No, but Gerard does, which is what is important."

"No one's taking my horse," Geordie said firmly.

"Gerard is essential to our cause, I'm afraid. You will be compensated, of course."

Geordie let it go, because the poor man wasn't thinking straight, to consider taking away a Scotsman's horse so as to placate a scroungy gypsy; he'd discover his mistake, if he were foolish enough to pull such a trick.

Instead, Geordie asked, "Now tell me of Marcello's allegiances, if you would."

"Marcello serves the Roman Catholic Church."

Geordie stared at him, thoroughly surprised. "He serves the Papist *Church*?"

"Yes. Our interests often align." The grey-eyed man paused, and then added fairly, "Not always, of course."

But Geordie found this idea nothing short of preposterous, and drew his brows together. "A strange sort of churchman, to be keeping company with a band of gypsies, and plotting to burn down the Alcazar."

But the grey-eyed man only offered in a mild tone, "I would not underestimate him. His particular Order has a long history of fighting in foreign lands."

Puzzled by the reference, Geordie ventured, "He's some sort of Crusader?"

"After a fashion. He belongs to the Knights of Malta— a group that absorbed the remnants of the old Knights Templar."

Slowly, Geordie shook his head in bemusement. "If someone had spun this tale to me by the campfire, I'd have said it was far too fanciful."

"Indeed. You need to be aware, Captain, that the girl may be making promises she will not keep."

Geordie let this slander pass, being as the spymaster didn't know Etta like Geordie knew Etta, despite the fact that his sum acquaintance with the lass was less than two days, and for a few snatches of conversation. "Nay; I'll not be foolish, sir."

The man's mouth twisted again. "A fond hope, but I understand this better than most."

Geordie made no response, as it seemed unlikely that the spymaster was the sort of man who'd allow a lass to keep him on a string. On the other hand, men were vulnerable to such things, as Geordie himself could now attest.

"I must go," the spymaster said.

"Aye, then. Good night," Geordie replied, and with no further ado, he turned to stride off toward the stables, and his bed.

CHAPTER 25

The next morning, the men rose early to eat a breakfast of cold ham and bread, smuggled-in by Ines in feed buckets. Geordie noted that their group now included two additions who'd arrived sometime during the night; Tornys had returned—with no explanation of where he'd been, since the rescue—and a big man named Petros, who readily helped himself to the food, and then sat with the others as though he was well-used to their company.

Covertly, Geordie observed the group as he ate, and was struck by something that seemed a bit unusual; the Romanies rarely seemed to converse. And they never joked or vied with one another, as men tended to do in a group. Of course, he was a *gadjo*, and his presence might affect how they behaved in front of him, but still, it seemed a little strange. And there was another thing; considering how they were supposedly members of different tribes, they all seemed very cohesive, with little bristling or posturing between the factions. Again, this was unusual, in Geordie's experience of men. He began to entertain the unwelcome suspicion that the group had a goal that was wholly their own, and that they were keeping this fact from him.

And because this possibility made him more than a little uneasy, when he rose to take a second helping, Geordie returned to settle-in beside Minos. He'd a few pressing questions in mind, and mayhap Minos would be willing to give him a straight answer, as he'd done in the past–rather surprisingly, all things considered.

"*Gadjo*," said Minos in greeting, and Geordie had the immediate impression that the other man was amused, because he was aware that Geordie was seeking information. "When do we go fishing, again?"

"We can't be seen, which is a damned shame," said Geordie, as he bent over his wooden trencher. "And I imagine once the Romanies have what they want, I'll never see hide nor hair of you again."

Minos paused to gaze upon him with reproach. "Ah, *gadjo*—you wound me."

But Geordie lowered his voice and cut to the nub, being as he didn't have much time. "There's two factions of Romanies, here, and they don't trust each other much." This wasn't a difficult conclusion to reach; Gerard and Gaston were clearly French, but all the others all had Greek-sounding names.

"Three factions," Minos corrected, as he lifted his flask to take a drink. "Four, if you count Marcello."

"I don't count Marcello," Geordie replied in a pointed manner.

Minos lowered his flask and nodded in diplomatic concession. "Three, then, because Adao is from his father's tribe—from Portugal."

Geordie eyed him sidelong, as he tore off a piece of bread. "Are they inclined to betray each other? Tell me now, before we start this operation."

Minos considered this. "No."

"Are they inclined to betray me?" This, of course, was the more important question.

The other man shrugged. "No; you are safe, *gadjo*. There is but one reason you are here, at all."

Geordie cocked his head. "My horse?"

With a twist to his mouth, the Romany man nodded. "*Si*; your horse. No one dares move against you."

Geordie nodded, and noted once again that Minos didn't seem to be taken-in like the others were, about the magic horse. He must not buy into the superstition, then, but was only humoring the others.

After chewing thoughtfully for a moment, Geordie ventured, "The French Romanies—the brothers—are helping the British, in exchange for Gerard's extraction from the Alcazar. But what do your people—the Greeks —want?"

"We are not from Greece," Minos explained in a patient tone. "Not for many years. Instead, we are from Spain—from Andalusia."

A bit impatiently, Geordie repeated, "All right, then; what does the Andalusian tribe want?"

Minos lifted his brows in surprise. "Vengeance, *gadjo* —is this not clear? The war has decimated our people."

"I don't think that's it," Geordie replied, as he tore off

another piece of bread. "Romanies aren't the sort to do vengeance—they don't dare."

Minos was silent, and so Geordie cut to the nub. "Here's my concern, friend; I can't help but think that I'm the one who's expendable, here, and I'd rather not go into a battle with troops who'd just as soon slit my throat." He nodded toward the group, silently eating their meal. "How do I know this lot can be trusted to obey orders? When all's said and done, I barely trust you."

Minos smiled. "You shouldn't trust any *Rom, gadjo*—I am surprised I must keep reminding you of this. But when the *baros* hear whispers that a revenge will be taken, they are all eager to take part." He paused. "It is not just Adao, who has lost everything."

"No rogue operations," Geordie warned. "Tell them; everyone has to agree to listen to command."

Minos seemed to find this very amusing, but he nodded gravely. "I will tell them, *gadjo*."

"Good; and let them know that as soon as everyone's finished eating, we'll gather-up and go over the operation. The faster we can muster, the more likely we'll succeed, since so many of the soldiers are away on the search for Adao."

"*Si*," Minos agreed, "I will tell them."

Since there seemed no time like the present, Geordie ventured, "You said that you'd tell me more about the Colonel's death, once I brought the Gypsy Queen to Gerard. Will you hold up your end of the bargain?"

The other man quirked his mouth. "You are very optimistic, *gadjo*."

But Geordie persisted, "I think Gerard was helping my old commander in some scheme, but I'll be damned if I can figure out why he would do it."

"Money," Minos replied, as though Geordie was a simpleton, not to have figured this out. "The Colonel promised Gerard a slice of the profits, from the operation."

This was plain-speaking, but Geordie kept his gaze on his trencher, and said in a level tone, "My commander wasn't a traitor, friend."

Minos shrugged. "He had little choice, *gadjo*. They threatened to kill his daughter, if he didn't cooperate." He paused. "And everyone knows that Rochon is a man who will kill children—and worse. *Un diablo más malvado.*"

Since this was an angle to the story he hadn't yet heard, Geordie decided to pretend as though this was possible—that the Colonel had been threatened into cooperating with the counterfeiting scheme. Not bloody likely, of course; the Colonel hadn't survived the Peninsular campaign by meekly buckling under, when the French made murderous threats. Instead, it seemed clear to him that the Colonel had feigned cooperation, but all the while was making a plan to thwart the enemy, and protect his daughter from any repercussions.

And it also seemed that Minos was unaware of the Colonel's "surety" plan with Gerard. So—if he didn't know, it meant that the French Romanies weren't being honest with the Andalusian Romanies, which wasn't much of a surprise, all in all. He'd have to hope Minos was right, and the two tribes were not inclined to betray each other—a unit had to work together, or it wouldn't survive the first foray.

"Thank you for telling me," Geordie said, and dusted off his breeches. "I appreciate it, friend."

"*De nada*," Minos replied, and returned his attention to his trencher.

CHAPTER 26

Whilst the others finished-up their meal, Geordie decided he should walk over to check on Jenny, who must be impatient with all this idleness—they hadn't had a restful day in years. He walked over to the far stall to see that Adao had given the mare a halter of oats, and was now untying it from her neck.

The horse turned her head so that Geordie could rub her forehead, and he cast an assessing eye over her. She looked none the worse for wear, and he nodded his thanks to Adao.

"You're spoiled, lass," he said to the horse. "You'd be the laughing-stock of the Fightin' Third, if they heard about your being the Queen of the Gypsies."

Adao smiled. "I did take the ribbons out of her mane and tail, *gadjo*."

"You're a good man, to help give her back her dignity. And I haven't had the chance to say 'well done' to you, laddie; your father would be that proud."

The boy flushed with pleasure, but shrugged. "It wasn't me, *gadjo*. The *Alkippa* goes where she wishes, and she does what she wants."

Diplomatically, Geordie offered, "Well, I'm glad she wished to fly over that gate with you; it was a sight to see, and I'll not forget it anytime soon."

Again, the boy smiled with pleasure. "*Si, gadjo;* I'll not forget it soon, either."

A good lad, thought Geordie; *he'd have made a good recruit, and—with a bit of seasoning—a good officer. I wonder what he does with himself, now; I think Gaston said that the guerrillas took him in, but there's no war to fight, anymore. Mayhap I can ask around, and find him a position in the Army, here.*

Marcello appeared at the entrance to the stall, and announced that everyone was ready to hear the plan.

"Have we a blacksmith?" asked Geordie, turning to join him.

"Yes; Petros is a blacksmith."

With a nod, Geordie strode over to where the other men were seated, awaiting their instructions, and began, "We'll spend the morning preparing the materials, and then we'll put the rockets together by this afternoon. We'll scout-out launching sites on the hills, and then attack around midnight, for maximum surprise."

He glanced around at the faces, solemnly watching him, and then his gaze rested on Petros. "I understand you're a blacksmith."

"*Si, señor,*" Petros replied. "And Adao learned much from his father."

"Good," said Geordie with approval, and privately

wondered how it was that Petros was familiar with Adao's abilities, if they were supposedly from different tribes.

Geordie continued, "I understand we have black powder in the smokehouse, and we'll need some launching sticks—a yard long, straight and strong; thumb-sized, or thereabouts. We'll also need materials for the fuses."

Marcello asked, "What type of material for the fuses?"

"Something that burns, but not too slowly, nor too quickly. The Army used silk thread, braided together, but it doesn't matter, as long as we can test it, so as to have a sense of the delta."

"What is the 'delta'?" asked Tornys.

Geordie explained, "It's the term they use for the time it takes for the fuse to burn down to the powder, once the rocket is airborne. If the delta's too fast, the rocket will explode in the air, and if it's too slow, the enemy will have a chance to extinguish the fuse, once it lands on the ground." He looked around at the intent faces. "We'll test out a few fuses ahead of time, because we need to be fairly certain of the delta, or it's all a wasted effort. And I trust I don't have to tell you that this is dangerous work; no smoking, or lighting a flame around the black powder."

"Why is the Padre needed?" Marcello asked, and it seemed to Geordie that the other man was a bit uneasy, with the idea that the Padre was to be given a task.

Geordie weighed how much to tell them. "The Padre has access to the Comandante, and so I will put him to use."

"An assassination?" asked Tornys, who seemed to think this a reasonable aim.

Firmly, Geordie shook his head. "Nay; we're sparing lives, if possible. Considering how the Spanish soldiers must feel with the *Afrancesados* in charge, they'll be less inclined to fight tooth and nail, if they can see that we are showing restraint."

This pronouncement was met with a dubious silence, and so Geordie thought it prudent to add in a joking tone, "Not to mention that the Padre might shrink, from having to murder the Comandante."

"I don't know if he's one to shrink from anything," Minos observed. "Not after Saragossa."

"But the Captain is right," Marcello said to the others. "We must avoid casualties, if possible, and make it clear that this is our aim. It will serve us well, in the long run."

It seemed clear that this point did not necessarily resonate with the Romanies, and so Geordie emphasized in a firm tone, "Everyone stays in their role, and obeys orders. We can't let this operation turn into a melee— that's how men get themselves killed." He gave them a commander's stare, until they all nodded in reluctant agreement.

"We can set up the forge here, outside the back stall," Marcello offered. "It will appear as though we are making shoes for the horses, as long as no one looks too closely. And we will ask the women to start braiding the fuses in the house."

"Good," said Geordie. "We'll do the packing of the rockets in the smokehouse, and that way we'll stay hidden, and we won't have to transport the powder."

As the others rose to go about their assigned tasks, Gaston remained behind, his attitude rather listless. "What is my role, *gadjo*? I am not a metal-worker."

Since they'd a moment alone, Geordie was sore-tempted to ask the man what he knew about his brother's dealings with the Colonel, but decided he didn't want to tip his hand—not yet. *Stay sharp, laddie,* he warned himself; *everyone is swimming in secrets.*

"We'll need to gather-up wood for the forge, as well as sticks for the rockets," Geordie suggested. "Don't act furtive, though—just casually gather it up."

The Romany man nodded, and Geordie watched him walk away.

There's a man who bears watching, Geordie concluded; he's not impressed by the magic horse, and—based on Etta's report–he isn't over-fond of his brother, either. In fact, he has the look of a man who's wracked—who's fighting demons–and that means, as a practical matter, that he'll not be very reliable in battle.

Suddenly, a querulous voice could be heard, calling to the house from the yard. "Ho, within. What's for breakfast? I've a mighty thirst."

"It appears that the Padre has arrived," Marcello said dryly.

Geordie asked, "Is it safe for me to go into the house? I'd like to speak with the Padre, and I can explain to the women what we'll need for the fuses."

"Go," said Marcello with a small smile. "I will send a signal, if there is any cause for alarm."

The kitchen door opened just as Geordie drew near, and he breathed in the welcome scent of bacon. "Good morning, Captain," said Ines, who bestowed on him a slow smile.

"Good morning, lass." He looked beyond her, to where the cook was filling a plate for the priest. "Good morning, Padre. I'd like a word."

"I'm not stopping you," said the priest, who made a smacking sound of appreciation at the cook, causing the plump woman to giggle. "You may suit yourself."

"May I make a plate for you, Captain?" Ines asked, with a hint of innuendo.

"I'd much appreciate it, lass," Geordie replied, and steered the priest toward the dining room before the man could smack his lips at Ines, too.

"Spoilsport," the Padre declared in a sour tone, as he settled in at the table. "Bloodless, you are–typical heathen."

But Geordie didn't have time to spar with the man,

and instead lowered his head. "I've a favor to ask of you, and I'll thank you to keep it under your hat."

The priest tilted his head, as he lifted his knife and fork. "That depends upon the ask, *señor.*"

"I need you to marry me to Etta. This evening, if possible."

Thoroughly surprised, the other man paused to stare at Geordie, and then he cackled with amusement. "She won't let you at her, without the vows?"

Geordie said in an even tone, "You will keep a civil tongue in your head, Padre, or I will knock it off your shoulders."

"*Si, si,*" the man said hurriedly, as he resumed his meal. "I was only joking; fah, no need to be so sensitive."

Geordie explained, "I've a pension, and I'd like her to have it, if I don't survive this."

The other man eyed him, as he ate. "And why wouldn't you survive this, *señor?*"

In a blunt manner, Geordie answered, "Because there's more going on, here, than what it seems, but damned if I know what it is. In my experience, that's not a good sign —there must be good reason that I'm being duped at every turn."

The priest snorted inelegantly. "You are dealing with gypsies, *señor.* They will dupe you for the sport of it."

Geordie bowed his head in acknowledgement. "Mayhap. But you can't tell anyone about the wedding, or there'll be no reward, coming your way."

With a gleam, the elderly man sopped up the last bit of butter with his bread. "What makes you think you can trust me more than the gypsies?"

"Not a blessed thing," Geordie admitted. But I need to be married, and fast, and you're the only Papist priest at hand."

His companion adopted a pious attitude. "I will do it, then—even though your poor soul is damned. It is the least I can do."

"Whatever you say, Padre," Geordie replied in a dry tone. "But draw up the marriage lines, all right and tight; it has to stick."

"*Si*." Cocking a sparse brow, the man added, "We will need a witness."

"I'll have one, never fear."

At this juncture, Ines came through the door, bearing Geordie's plate. "Your breakfast, Captain."

She set the heaping plate before him, and Geordie lifted his knife and fork in appreciation. "Thank you, lass —reminds me of home; I've not eaten so well in many a day."

Rather to his surprise, the serving girl slid into the chair beside him, and idly picked up a slice of his bacon in her slender fingers. "Is that so? When will you return to your home, Captain?"

"I canno' say, lass—it all depends." He paused to smile at her, but kept his words as vague as possible, because he recognized a lure, when it was being thrown, and was well-used to avoiding them.

Ines broke the bacon apart so as to eat the pieces; popping them into her mouth one at a time. "Is there anyone who waits for you, there?"

Out of the corner of his eye, Geordie saw the Padre smile into his coffee cup. "The neighbor's daughter was angling," Geordie readily confessed. "But her people are farmers, and I wouldn't know one end of a plow from another."

"Ah. What will you do, instead?" the girl asked, her sidelong gaze resting on him, as she ate another piece.

Geordie shrugged slightly, and lifted another forkful. "Well, my horse seems to think I should stay in Spain for a while, and she hasn't been wrong, yet."

Ines smiled, and leaned in a bit. "I am glad to hear it. Perhaps—"

But whatever she was going to say was cut off, as the Senora entered the room, with Etta by her side— the lass's head held high, and her cheeks tinged with pink. Whilst Geordie recognized a lure, he also recognized a jealous woman, when he saw one, and so he immediately rose to his feet to address her. "Miss," he said respectfully. "Will you join us for breakfast?"

"I'm ready for another plate," the Padre said agreeably.

"I understand you require our assistance, Captain," the Senora replied. "Perhaps while we eat, you can explain to us what is needed."

"Readily," said Geordie, who couldn't like the openness of the discussion, with the cook and the servants within earshot. "I've a sewing project for you— making blankets for wounded veterans."

"You may trust everyone in the house, *señor,*" the Senora said calmly, as she allowed him to pull out her chair, and see her seated.

"If you say, ma'am," Geordie replied. It seemed he'd

little choice in the matter, and he could only hope that it was true.

"Women's work," the Padre scoffed, as he pushed out his own chair. "If you need me, I'll be in the kitchen."

Geordie promptly seated Etta in the Padre's vacated chair, which left her next to Ines. As the two young women greeted each other politely, Geordie hoped the serving girl would behave herself—a minx, she was, and not unwilling to stir up trouble, if he was any judge such things. In fact, it was a bit odd, that the rather stern Senora hadn't rebuked the girl for seating herself at the table, and helping herself to a guest's meal.

Standing at the table's end, Geordie explained to the women, "We'll need to make lengths of braided silk—or braided cotton twine." He was reluctant to call them 'fuses' outright; the less said about their purpose, the better. For that matter, he realized he'd never been given the Senora's name, and figured that this was not an oversight; the woman risked much, by housing and feeding them. He'd the sense, though, that despite her age and her dignified manner, she wouldn't have hesitated to take up arms herself, like those women in Guarda, who'd bravely tried to hold the town, all on their own.

"Only tell us what must be done," the elderly woman said, "and we will do it."

Geordie nodded. "It is important that each length be consistent—the same materials in each, and the same thickness throughout." He held up his fingers, to demonstrate. "About yea big. We'll need to know how much time it takes to burn from one end to the other, and it should be the same for each."

The Senora nodded. "What length, do you wish?"

"A yard or so. Once we have the timing figured, I can cut them shorter as needed."

"How quickly do you need them?"

Geordie tilted his head. "As soon as may be. If I could have a dozen by noon, that would be much-appreciated. We can add from there, but at least we can get started on a stockpile."

The woman rose. "I will fetch the materials." As she turned to leave, she added, "If you would assist me, Ines."

With good grace, the serving girl rose to follow her mistress, which left Geordie thankfully alone with Etta.

CHAPTER 28

Without hesitation, Geordie slid into the chair next to Etta's, and bent his head. "I've got to speak fast, lass, and I'm that sorry to be so abrupt. We'll need to get married, all quiet-like. The Padre will do it, and I'll come by again tonight, as I did last night. You can't tell anyone, though. I'm sorry for it, but it's important that no one else know."

The clear green eyes searched his in alarm. "What has happened? Are you in danger?"

"Nay, lass," he replied, and hoped that this was true. "But it's the same as though I'm going into battle, and I'd like to feel that everything's sorted out. I've a pension, and—and an inheritance, coming my way."

"Do not say this," she admonished him, her brows drawn together. "Do not."

In the face of her dismay, he placed a comforting hand over hers, and tempered his words. "No—you're right; there's no need to rush things. I must sound barking mad, but it's only that I think like a soldier thinks, and sometimes I forget that everyone else doesn't."

There was a small silence, whilst she regarded him, her brow knit. "May my brother attend?"

With mixed emotions, Geordie noted that—whilst she seemed willing to do the deed—she didn't seem to understand the urgent request for secrecy. "Nay, lass, I'm afraid not. After all, he'll not be best pleased with such a hole-in-corner affair, and that I haven't done it properly, by asking his permission first."

With a small smile, she turned her hand, so as to hold his fingers in hers. "Marcello will understand," she said gently. "He is someone who trusts my judgment."

There was a small, significant pause, and Geordie slowly let out a breath. "As do I, lass. If you think it best, by all means, have him stand up with you." *Lord,* he thought; *so much for operational secrecy—you're in a sorry state, laddie.* On the bright side, she'd agreed to wed him, and everything else seemed paltry in comparison. She was a bonny, bonny lass, and so even if she brought about his doom, he'd go to his grave a happy man.

The lady of the house returned with a basket of silks, and Geordie rose to take his leave. "Might I have a word, ma'am?"

She nodded. "Certainly, *señor*." After instructing Ines to begin laying out the strands of silk on the dining table, she stepped into the parlor.

Geordie stood with his back to the doorway, so that he blocked any view of their actions, and then pulled the folded mortgage document out from within his waistcoat, to hold it flat against his chest. "I've a favor to ask, ma'am. The Padre will be marrying me to Etta tonight, if you will stand as a witness." He paused. "You can't tell anyone, though. It's very important."

He was somewhat surprised to see an amused light come into the older woman's eyes, but in a grave tone, she agreed, "I will be happy to stand as witness to your marriage, *señor*. I have some experience, in this."

"And there's another favor, hard on the first one." He tapped his forefinger on the parchment. "I'd ask you to hold something for me, all secret-like. If it doesn't go well for me, I need you to give it to my wife, since it would be hers. I'm sorry to ask, but again, it's important that no one else know of it."

With a quick movement, the woman deftly snatched-up the parchment, and tucked it in her shawl. "*Si*; I will do as you ask, *señor*."

"Much appreciated." In a louder voice, he added, "Right, then; if you could send Ines out to the stables with the fuses when they're ready; I should try to stay out of sight."

"*Bueno*," the woman agreed with a regal nod, and calmly moved to return to the dining room.

As he pulled on his hat, Geordie nodded his appreciation to the cook, and then headed out the kitchen door. All in all, this seemed the best possible solution to his current dilemma. From what he'd gleaned, it seemed that the Colonel had made Geordie his 'surety' in the event his plan—whatever it was—went awry, but Geordie hadn't played his part, and instead of marrying the man's daughter and laying claim to the mines, he'd lingered here in Spain, asking uncomfortable questions.

And then, the next thing he knew, he was being drafted to rescue the very counterfeiter who'd created the mortgage—this tale about the magic horse being an obvious tarradiddle. Therefore, it seemed clear to Geordie that the silver mines must be what was motivating the gypsies—they *had* to be, since nothing else made a lick o' sense. But it also seemed clear that the spymaster and Marcello weren't aware that he held the mortgage—only the Romanies were aware.

And, truth to tell, this seemed rather ominous. Certainly, he could be forgiven for wondering if there was a Romany plan afoot to seize the mortgage, and then have Geordie meet the same fate as the Colonel. They were gypsies, after all, and he wouldn't put it past them. Now that the Colonel was dead, it must be mighty tempting for Gerard to lay claim to the mines for himself—he was a counterfeiter, after all, and could probably change the document in a trice.

In fact, Geordie would be inclined to suspect exactly such a plot, were it not for one notable fact: Gerard's genuine distress upon beholding Geordie, here in Spain. It hadn't seemed to him that the Romany man was feigning his reaction, and indeed, even Marcello had noticed. Gerard was sore-bothered that Geordie—and his mortgage—were still here, with no one the wiser, and that reaction didn't seem in keeping with a plot to put a period to Geordie's existence.

Nevertheless, it made him gravely uneasy, because even if Gerard meant to hold faith with the Colonel's plan, there was yet another danger, atop that one. The mortgage had been created to thwart the enemy's plan to fund their next war, which meant it was a dire threat to some very dangerous people. If those dangerous people somehow gained knowledge of its existence, Geordie's life would be forfeit without a second's hesitation.

Therefore, he'd decided that the prudent course was to set up his own surety, as best he could; he'd trust no one with the whole story, hope the Spanish lady held faith, and let the mortgage land in Etta's hands, if it came down to it. Her brother Marcello seemed a knowing one, and hopefully he could be trusted to sort out the Colonel's plan to defeat the enemy—it was definitely beyond Geordie's ken to grasp it, since nothing that was happening seemed to add up. They all wanted him to believe he'd been included in this adventure on account of his mare, but he was a hard-headed Scot, and recognized a bamboozle when he heard one. It *had* to be about the silver mines; without them, Geordie was just another soldier with a passing knowledge of rocketry.

To the good, he was fast-unraveling the circumstances that surrounded the Colonel's death, and he'd managed to snag himself a fine wife in the process, so it was not all briars without a few roses.

Whistling softly, he headed toward the stables.

CHAPTER 29

The rhythmic tones of Petros' hammer kept a steady beat in the background, as the big man fashioned the metal cylinders that would house the rockets. Adao had readily assumed an assistant's role, and Geordie could hear them speak with an easy camaraderie, as the two worked together. Again, Geordie had the impression they were well-familiar, which didn't hold together with the story he'd been told.

He'd called all the other Romanies together to discuss the assembly of the rockets, and explained in low tones, "We're waiting on the fuses, but the first batch should be ready soon. For the attack, we'll split into two teams, to be stationed on either side of the Alcazar—we'll go up into the hills to scout out the launching places, ahead of time. Then we'll wait until midnight; my team will launch the first rocket, which will be the signal for the other team to launch. If we keep the rockets coming from two different sides, it will add to the confusion."

Tornys, who'd been assigned to the other team,

listened intently. "How can we be certain you have launched?"

Geordie smiled. "There speaks a man who hasn't seen a rocket in action. Don't worry; there'll be no mistaking it." He paused, and met everyone's gaze around the circle. "We're out to destroy the buildings, with as few casualties as possible. To this end, we'll first target the Armory, so as to destroy their stockpile. That should set off some rare fireworks, and we'll wait a few minutes, so as to allow everyone to come out, before launching a second wave at the other buildings, and the barracks. With any luck, we'll be able to clear out, and get away before they scout-out our positions. It would probably be best if we don't reconvene here, but scatter, instead. That way, the people who have helped us can say they'd no idea what we were about, if they are questioned."

"A very good point," Marcello agreed.

"No one approaches the Alcazar, during the attack," Geordie cautioned. "We don't want any hostages, and we don't want to put any of you in danger from the rocket attack—the rockets tend to be unpredictable."

He then waited a beat, to see if Marcello would add anything. He hadn't forgot about the supposed treasure-casket that Marcello was set to retrieve for the British spymaster—even though neither man had spoken a word about it to him. But both the Padre and Minos seemed to believe this was indeed his goal, and so it stood to reason that Marcello must have operatives within the Alcazar— the surgeon, for one. It was the logical assumption, and it would further explain why the man was reluctant to kill any personnel with the initial rocket attack.

But Marcello added no comment, and so Geordie continued, "We'll load the black powder into the casings as soon as we get the fuses—Gaston has gathered-up the launching-sticks, and I'll need a couple of men with steady hands to do it with me in the smokehouse. No smoking, no lanterns."

He didn't mention that he didn't want Gaston involved—he'd think of an excuse, closer to the time. When the Romany man had handed over the sticks, his hand had trembled a bit, and he hadn't met Geordie's eyes. *Craves a drink, he does,* thought Geordie, who'd seen these symptoms many a time, and in many a soldier. *Best leave him out of anything important.*

Geordie continued, "We'll need a few candles, as well as plenty of lucifers. If it's raining or windy, we'll need to hold a steady flame, to light the fuses."

"The Padre can bring lucifers, when he comes by this afternoon," Marcello said. "And we will request candles from the house."

"Good. As soon as the fuses are here, we'll set to work."

Shortly thereafter, Ines smuggled-in the first batch of fuses in a feed bucket, and informed Geordie that—at their current length—they burned for two minutes.

"That's grand, lass," he said with satisfaction. "I'll cut them down, so that the delta is shorter. A shame we can't test it out ahead of time, but that would give the game away. We can always adjust, during the attack."

"How many rockets will we shoot?" asked Tornys.

"Two dozen is the minimum, I reckon. There will be

misfires, and some that will get put out by the enemy, before they explode."

Gathering up the metal cylinders along with the fuses, Geordie choose Petros and Tornys to accompany him into the smokehouse, and then begin the work of packing the black powder into the rocket cylinders. It wasn't ideal, in that it was necessarily dark and airless, but they couldn't risk assembling them in the stables, and so Georgie demonstrated as best he could, with the other two men huddled close around him in the dimness—they dared not light a flame.

Over the next couple of hours, an arsenal began to take shape, as a dozen rockets were carefully packed into canvas bags, ready to be transported up into the hills. As they awaited the next batch of fuses, Geordie walked over to stand in the doorway for a moment, his hands on his hips—it was sweaty, close work in the smokehouse, and he was grateful for a breath of air. Almost immediately, the kitchen door opened to reveal Etta, her pretty head wrapped closely in a shawl, as she stepped down the stoop with a feed bucket in her hand. With an inward smile, he thought, *Will you look at that; I believe the lass is longing for a word.*

He smiled in greeting, as he moved to take the feed bucket from her hand. "Dinna come too close, lass; I'll need a good dunk in the river, when I'm through, here."

"Yes; a 'dunk' sounds very appealing." A bit self-consciously, she then added, "Geordie," as though she was getting used to saying his name.

To put her at ease, he asked, "Can you swim, lass?"

With a smile, she nodded. "I can. From when I was very little."

Geordie grinned down at her, as he ran a forearm across his forehead. "We'll go swimming soon, then—the sooner, the better; I'm mighty sick of staying indoors."

"I am, also," she agreed, and then repeated his phrase, as though to test it out, "The sooner, the better."

"You speak English very well," he noted, and then joked, "Better than me, almost—and it's a good thing, else we'd have a hard time communicating."

"Your Spanish is very good," she offered, as though to placate him. "Here—I brought a flask of water."

"Much appreciated." He accepted the flask, and thought, *So; the lass speaks a few languages.* This didn't come as much of a surprise; Marcello spoke like someone who was well-educated, and so it stood to reason that his sister would be, too. Between the two of them, they didn't make very convincing gypsies, but this was a good thing; he'd known almost from the first that he was being hoodwinked, and it had helped him to stay sharp. Not that he'd been very sharp around the lassie, of course— hopefully she wasn't leading him astray. He didn't think so, though; he'd duly noted, during their conversation, that she couldn't seem to keep her gaze from the damp shirt that stretched across his chest. *I believe this poor lassie craves a bedding,* he thought, as he tilted back the flask, and drank deeply. *It's a right blessing that I'm just the man for the job.*

She seemed inclined to linger, but Geordie was on a schedule, and so he handed back the flask. "Thank you, lass—and please convey my thanks to the others, too. Even Ines," he teased, and cocked a brow at her.

She laughed, and the dimple appeared in her cheek. "I will—even Ines." She added in a low voice, "I told my brother." And then, in the event he'd forgot, she added, "About the wedding."

"Good," he said, and decided he didn't want to ask about Marcello's reaction. "I've got the Padre lined up, and we'll get the deed done after dark, when everyone's busy preparing for the attack."

She nodded, and made no reply.

He tilted his head. "Have you heard any more conversations I should know about?"

"No." She made a wry mouth, and added, "Although Ines speaks of you. I think she teases me, because she knows that I—that you and I—"

"Did you tell her I'm spoken-for?" he asked, his eyes wide.

She couldn't hide a smile, and chided him gently, "No. It is a secret, Geordie—you mustn't forget."

"Not a secret for long," he assured her. In a more serious tone, he added, "Do you think Ines can't be trusted? If you've a worry, you must let me know."

"No—I don't think she is a 'worry'," Etta replied thoughtfully. "Everyone treats her with much respect—when she speaks with the Senora, the Senora listens carefully."

He nodded, thinking about how the Padre had told him, right from the first, that Ines could be trusted. It seemed obvious that the serving girl brought information from her post within the Alcazar, and so it stood to reason that they relied on her.

In parting, he advised, "The Senora strikes me as a long-headed woman, and so I'd ask that you stick to her side, from here on out. No more visits, Etta; you're to stay within the house, and stay safe."

There was a small silence, whilst she regarded him steadily, and Geordie belatedly remembered that the lass didn't much like to be ordered about. But rather than remind him of this, she only replied in a grave tone, "If you say, Geordie," and he'd the brief impression that she was mightily amused—her eyes were alight, despite her best efforts.

"Your eyes are a rare treat, lass," he felt compelled to say. "Like sunlight through new leaves."

"We must go swimming," she replied with some intensity. "The sooner, the better."

CHAPTER 30

Their task completed, the three men left the smokehouse to return to the stables, where Ines once again used feed buckets to smuggle-in the midday meal. Geordie watched the serving girl, as she doled out the offerings, and thought about what Etta had said—about how the Senora listened, when Ines spoke. It made him realize something that seemed a bit strange; Ines was a comely lass—and apparently willing to take a tumble at the slightest suggestion—but he'd never seen any of these men attempt to put it to the touch.

He lowered his gaze to his meal, and chewed thoughtfully. Come to think of it, everyone here seemed almost deferential to the lass, as though they respected her—although why a group of gypsies would respect a kitchen slattern was unclear. Was she kin to them, mayhap? That seemed unlikely; she appeared to be a fixture in this household, and didn't look to be a gypsy lass—although the various tribes that were represented here didn't much look like each other, either. It was yet another puzzle in what seemed an unending heap of them.

Minos had settled-in beside him, and so Geordie decided to do a bit of probing. "Who do you have, within the Alcazar?"

Minos looked up in surprise. "I have no one within the Alcazar, *gadjo*. Why would you think this?"

Geordie weighed what to say. "Someone does, I reckon. If not you, Marcello, mayhap."

Minos shrugged, and addressed his bowl. "If you say so, *gadjo*."

Lifting his face to contemplate the rafters overhead, Geordie mused aloud, "I'd give another tooth, just to have a unit of British soldiers at my back. I can't trust a soul around me."

The Romany man chuckled in amusement. "Ah, *gadjo;* you forget that you can trust the *Alkippa*."

Readily, Geordie agreed. "That's true; if I'd my druthers, I'd trust my Jenny more than the lot of you, thrown together. And that reminds me; Gerard's demand that he be given my mare makes no sense. He doesn't want to be King of the Gypsies—that was only a round tale, to dupe Marcello and the British spymaster. You told me yourself that the gypsies don't have kings and queens. And besides that, even if he wished, Gerard knows he can't just seize the *Alkippa*, and keep her for himself. According to all of you, she 'goes where she wishes, and does what she wants.'"

"You mock me, *gadjo*, but it is the truth," Minos replied. "In fact, the *Alkippa* made it clear that she did not like what was planned, and so the plan was changed, to accommodate her wishes."

Ah-ha, thought Geordie; *now we are finally getting somewhere.* "What was the plan, and how was it changed?"

"I am tired of keeping track of my lies," the other man admitted. "And so, I will not tell you."

Geordie had to chuckle, and he spread his hands on his knees. "Fair enough; I'll go over to the main house to speak with Gerard, tonight, before we go on the operation. I'll see if I can get a straight answer out of him—I'd rather not be playing blind man's bluff with a pack of gypsies." He'd already decided that he needed to hear some straight answers from the counterfeiter, before the operation went forward, so that he could assess his own level of danger. Not to mention that a visit to speak with Gerard would serve as a good excuse to get into the house for his secret wedding.

Minos smiled into his bowl as he scraped up the dregs. "Gerard is no longer here, *gadjo*."

"Gerard's *gone*?" Whilst Geordie regarded Minos with surprise for a moment, he decided—on second thought—there was no real reason to be surprised. The British spymaster had extracted Gerard—who was now supposedly dead—and so it made sense that the valuable Romany man would be spirited away somewhere safe, presumably well-away from Napoleon's counterfeiting operation.

"What's to eat?" called out a querulous voice from the stable yard. "And I've a few wineskins, to pass around."

"No spirits," Geordie immediately cautioned the other

men, as the Padre appeared at the stable door. "Everyone needs to have a clear head." In particular, he didn't want to tempt Gaston; more than a few operations had been compromised by a man who'd been drinking a bit too deep.

"Spoilsport," said the Padre without rancor, as he handed his horse to Adao. "I'll go within, then, where my wine is welcome."

"I've a task for you," Geordie informed him. "See me, before you leave."

"Let's go in with him," Marcello suggested, as he rose to head toward the door. "I want to make certain he understands the sequence of events."

"*Si*—be careful not to shoot me with your rockets," the Padre warned. "I am not ready for heaven, just yet."

"More like heaven's not ready for you," Geordie replied, as he willingly joined the other two men.

"I'll not listen to your heresy, *señor*. Come; I am hungry."

As the three men walked across the stable yard toward the house, Geordie asked Marcello, "What's the status of the search for Adao?"

"Our people have laid false trails toward the north," the other man replied. "The Alcazar search party continues to hear reports of a boy on a fine black mare, just ahead of them, and so the Comandante is urging them on, especially since Rochon is due to arrive here at any moment."

"I can't blame the Comandante," Geordie remarked. "I wouldn't want to be in his shoes, with his valuable prisoner dead, and nothing to show for it."

"Rochon will not be best-pleased," Marcello agreed. "But he cannot move too openly, for the same reasons we cannot."

"Aye," Geordie agreed thoughtfully. "He has no official authority, so I suppose he can't punish anyone outright—although if everyone's as afraid of him as you say, that hardly matters."

"More like anyone who fails Rochon will simply disappear," said the Padre sourly. "I've known of a few, myself."

"Certainly, he cannot blame the Comandante for what happened," Marcello pointed out. "Which was one of the reasons the rescue was staged as it was; no one could have anticipated the bride's brother murdering the groom."

"You've never been to Scotland, obviously," Geordie replied.

"No matter—it is all to the good," the Padre declared. "The Comandante will be in a state, and so he will overdrink my excellent wine."

"Aye," Geordie agreed. "If he's befuddled for the attack, it's to our benefit. But there's an additional task I'll ask of you."

The Padre cocked a wary eyebrow, and warned, "Nothing where I risk myself."

"Nay; I ask only that when you visit the Comandante this afternoon, you bring along two casks that are filled with black powder—new casks, they can't be wet. There are wooden barrels stored along the north wall of the Armory; if you will set the casks behind those barrels, next to the wall, I would much appreciate it."

The other two considered this for a moment, and Marcello said, "Added firepower, to breach the Armory walls."

Geordie nodded. "That, and it will confound the enemy, to have additional explosions that are not seen to be from the rockets."

"A very good plan," said the Padre, rubbing his hands. "I will do it."

"Many thanks," said Geordie. "It's a stroke of luck that you go in with the casks today; they'll not suspect you of sabotage."

"Nor should they," the priest replied, very much upon his dignity. "I am a man of God, *señor*."

They came to the house's back stoop, and Geordie paused to ask, "Do you mind if I wash at the pump?" It had occurred to him that the two men who accompanied him into the house were the very two who would be needed for his wedding, which had apparently been moved forward.

"Certainly," said Marcello. "But I will warn you; the Senora asks that we help to move her bedstead, upstairs. It is quite heavy, and the task will require several strong men."

"Willingly," said Geordie, who couldn't suppress a smile.

The priest cackled, and gave Geordie a sly glance. "Such luck, to have a bedstead so close at hand."

"You're to keep a civil tongue in your head," Geordie reminded him, as he pulled his shirt over his head.

CHAPTER 31

he three men had just settled-in at the table in the kitchen—again, the Padre openly flirting with the cook—when the Senora appeared in the doorway. "If I could ask for your assistance, *señores*."

"Of course," Marcello replied.

As they trooped up the stairs, it occurred to Geordie that Marcello would soon be his brother, and this might raise a few problems, in that Geordie had the very strong feeling there was more to the man than met the eye. The spymaster had said that Marcello served the Papist church in his doings, but Geordie had never caught the sense that there was any particular alliance, 'twixt Marcello and the Padre—no awareness, between the two —and in fact, it didn't seem that the Padre respected the other man much. Not that the Padre seemed to respect anyone, of course, but Etta said that the Padre would know where to find her, which seemed to indicate the two men were indeed allied, in some way. It was hard to fathom; the Padre seemed to personify all that was wrong with the Papist church, and you'd think Marcello wouldn't fraternize with such a poor example. *Stay sharp, laddie,* Geordie warned himself. *If Marcello's to be family, you may have to cover for him, whatever his allegiances.*

They filed into the Senora's bedchamber, and Geordie's gaze was immediately drawn to Etta, who was seated by the window and sewing, supposedly, although —on second look—her needle wasn't threaded.

Nervous, the lass is, he thought with a pang; and small blame to her.

He immediately strode across the room and knelt at her feet, gently taking up her hands in his. In a low voice, he said, "I'll not press you, lass. You can think on it, and we can do the deed at some other time."

An expression of alarm rose up in her eyes. "Do you wish to wait?" she whispered. "Tell me the truth, Geordie."

"Not for a second."

"Nor do I." She squeezed the hands that held hers.

"Ouch," he said, as the needle jabbed him.

"Oh—oh, your pardon." She met his eyes, her own filled with amusement, and he'd the immediate and profound sense that all was right with the world. *I've no idea who she is—she could indeed be the Queen of the Gypsies, for all I know, but damned if we aren't meant for each other.*

Geordie rose to his feet, and pulled her up beside him. "Buckle us up, Padre," he directed cheerfully. "On the double."

"Typical, to take a sacrament so lightly," the priest groused, although he stepped forward to stand before them, and dutifully pulled a small prayer book from his cassock's deep pocket.

Marcello and the Senora moved into place beside the bride and groom, and the priest began to recite the ceremony—unfamiliar to Geordie, who was used to the Book of Common Prayer, but all in all, the basics were the same. He held his bride's hand in his, and listened intently—he needed the lass to know that he took it seriously, even though it was a thrown-together ceremony. He'd attended many such, on the eve of battle, but the lass wasn't a field bride, and it was a shame that she was to be treated as one. No doubt she'd been dreaming of a proper wedding, with flowers and silks; he'd have to make it up to her, assuming he survived this day.

It came time to recite their vows, and the priest asked them to face each other, and repeat the phrases as he said them. Willingly, Geordie began, "I, George Gordon Venables, take thee—" here he paused, nonplussed, since he wasn't certain what her full name was.

The dimple appeared on her cheek, and she prompted, "Margaretta Maria—"

"Margaretta Maria," he repeated.

But she continued, "Catalina Felicia—"

Gamely, Geordie added, "Catalina Felicia."

"Testaferrata—"

"Testaferrata."

"Della Fonseca."

"Della Fonseca," Geordie finished, making a mighty effort to control his acute dismay at this litany of names. *You're in way over your head, laddie, and this is exactly what you get for not marrying the neighbor's platter-faced daughter, and staying home to try your hand at farming.*

Etta recited her own vows, her eyes shining, and then the priest asked, "Is there a ring?"

"I have none left," the Senora explained in a dry tone. My apologies."

"I'll buy you a proper ring, lass, first chance we get," Geordie assured Etta.

"I now pronounce you man and wife," the Padre finished, and snapped his prayer book closed. "*Deo Gratias.*"

As the others repeated the phrase, Geordie gathered his new bride into his arms and said into her ear, I'll kiss you proper, lass, when we haven't an audience."

"The sooner, the better," she replied in her own happy whisper, and he chuckled. Lord alive, but she was a bonny, bonny lass, and if he couldn't navigate the both of them through this maze in one piece, he didn't deserve her in the first place.

"I have drawn-up the marriage lines," said the Senora. "If you will sign, please."

After they'd performed this task, Geordie thanked them all, and then he and Marcello duly moved the bedstead, and returned down the stairs. As they re-seated themselves at the kitchen table, Marcello leaned in to ask in a low voice, "Shall we speak of Etta's dowry?"

"No, brother," Geordie said bluntly. "I've a feeling it's not something that I'll want to hear." *The lass had a dozen names, for the holy love of Christ.*

Marcello smiled dryly. "Some other time, then."

Geordie nodded, and refrained from comment. It

seemed obvious that his new wife was some sort of nob, masquerading as a gypsy, and the only thing that salvaged the whole situation was she wasn't an English nob. Or at least, as far as he knew—he'd cross that bridge if he came to it. Reminded, he advised Marcello, "I've an Army pension, just so you know. And an inheritance, too —don't overlook it."

Marcello seemed amused, as he gravely nodded, which gave Geordie the uneasy impression that the man was humoring him. *They're rich*, he decided. *But I can't very well hold it against them; they're kin, now.*

The Padre interrupted, leaning down as he stood behind them, and placed a hand around each man's shoulder. In a low voice, he offered, "A shame, that we've nothing to toast your happiness, *señor*."

"No drinking, before you handle the casks," Geordie warned. "The last needful thing is for you to blow yourself up, and give the game away."

"I am a rock," the Padre retorted, very much affronted. "I survived Saragossa, sir."

"Let's hope this assignment is nowhere near as troublesome," Geordie replied. "Try not to get yourself shot."

"I've been shot thrice," the priest scoffed. "Another would be as nothing."

"Don't give me reason to test it out," Geordie warned.

While it was still daylight, Geordie took a scouting party into the hills, to choose the launching sites. This proved to be no easy feat, because the sites had to be within range of the Alcazar, in a place that was clear overhead, but had at least some cover, because the launch sites would be vulnerable as soon as the enemy figured out what was happening. It was fortunate that the rockets could be moved elsewhere, in the event they were fired upon; it was a huge advantage, to have the devices mounted on their own launching sticks, and Congreve's idea had changed the balance of warfare.

There was the added complication that the Alcazar's soldiers were scouring the countryside, looking for Adao, but again, Marcello assured him that there were few searchers in their immediate area, which was why they should strike quickly, before the remainder of the soldiers returned empty-handed.

As the men quietly threaded their way through the

trees, Geordie's thoughts were necessarily a bit grim, because yet again, he'd realized something that seemed a bit ominous—something in addition to the first ominous thing, which was that the gypsies might be willing to kill him, so as to seize the silver mines.

But—after a bit of reflection—he now had a second concern, that seemed even more ominous than the first. Both Minos and the Padre had hinted that everyone would rather this Rochon fellow were dead, for his sins, and it occurred to Geordie that there was nothing like the chaos of a bombardment to give someone an opportunity to strike the man down, all quiet-like, with no one to take the blame. No one, that was, unless the British spymaster decided that Geordie should be at hand, as a convenient scapegoat for such an egregious breach of the peace agreement. After all, a rocket attack couldn't be easily explained away as the vengeful action of a ragtag group of Romanies—no; instead here was Captain Venables, who—lo and behold—had been telling everyone that he was looking to avenge his commander's death. Captain Venables, who was well-versed in the making of rockets. In truth, it would answer nicely.

Geordie didn't like to think that the spymaster would turn him such a dastardly trick, but from what he'd heard, the man was ruthless in his pursuits, and wielded a lot of power. A retired Army Captain with no supporters could be easily sacrificed, if it meant Napoleon's next war effort would be crippled, before it gained any momentum.

It was yet another reason to be wary—another reason atop all the other reasons—and indeed, it would be a more believable explanation as to why Geordie had been recruited by the Romanies, than the tale about his supposed magic horse. They were acting at the direction of the spymaster, who needed a scapegoat for when the smoke cleared.

Although—although to be fair, the spymaster himself didn't seem to know a lot about what was unfolding. For instance, he seemed to truly believe that Gerard sought to be King of the Gypsies, and that the man needed Geordie's horse, to achieve this aim. And the spymaster didn't seem to know anything about the Colonel's mortgage, or the threats against the Colonel's daughter that had prompted the mortgage-surety-plan, to begin with.

All in all, it was hard to fathom—there was little doubt that the spymaster was as clever as they come, but Geordie had the sense that the man truly didn't know that the Romanies were hoodwinking him, at every turn.

Which only led back to Geordie's sense of unease; if the spymaster wasn't controlling this operation, who was? And why? Mayhap the real reason had yet to be revealed, and it wasn't a good one for Geordie's continued health and well-being.

In light of these rather troubling thoughts, he decided to fall into step beside Petros, who he hadn't spoken with much, but who'd worked silently and efficiently in making the casings for the rockets. Since the big man hadn't been with the group as long, it might be possible for Geordie to bluff his way into winkling-out some more information.

In an affable tone, Geordie began, "That was good

work, today. A shame we canno' test them out, beforehand—we'll have to hope for the best."

The man nodded. "*Si, señor.*"

"You seemed well-able; have you ever worked on rockets, before?"

"No, *señor.*"

Geordie cocked his head, and advised, half-joking, "You have to be careful not to share what you've learned, friend. Adao's tribe would be mighty happy, if they could use them to wipe-out the *Calé*. We can't allow the rockets to fall into the wrong hands."

Smiling at his tone, Petros nodded. "I understand. I will be careful."

Geordie instructed, "You'll be at the alternate launch site, and I'll ask you to keep a sharp eye, and make certain no one else gets sloppy; if any one of the rockets goes off during transport up the hill, we'll be sunk."

The other man nodded. "*Si.*"

Geordie added, "We'll have to transport them on our backs, I'm afraid. They'll be heavy, but a pack animal might startle, and cause problems when you light the fuses. In the Army, we had some mules who were solid as a rock, to carry munitions, and I wish we had one now. The gates of hell could open up beneath their feet, and they'd still hold their position, and wouldn't turn a hair. My Jenny, too—pluck to the backbone, even with the cannons firing all around her."

The other man glanced at him. "*Si,* she is a fine mare, *señor.* How long have you had her?"

"Since Badajoz."

"Oh?" The other man raised his brows. "She is older than she seems, then."

"Aye."

As they continued their trek up the hill, Geordie considered the fact that Petros was not only unfamiliar with the gypsy tribes, he was also not aware that the mare was anything special. And—come to think of it—the man called him *señor,* and the Romanies never called him *señor,* *they* called him *gadjo*—whatever that meant; something a bit insulting, he'd the sense.

So; Petros was not a Romany, but what did it mean? Could the two men—Petros and Tornys—be assassins for the spymaster, infiltrating the gypsy troop so as to go after Rochon? It didn't make much sense, since the attack was going to be launched from outside of the fort, instead of from within. And, if they were only posing as Romanies, it would mean that the other Romanies were aware of the masquerade, and willing to treat them as though they were fellow Romanies. Which seemed hard to believe; if there was a covert assassination plot afoot, it seemed unlikely that the spymaster would trust a band of gypsies with the details of the plan—Geordie himself wouldn't trust any one of them as far as he could throw them.

None of it made sense—in fact, it was making less and less sense, the more he found out about these people. *You're in over your head, laddie,* he thought yet again, *and if you'd any sense at all, you'd gather up the lass and head for the hills.*

The only problem with this sensible plan seemed to be that there was little chance of escaping; whoever was behind this carefully-contrived plan was very clever, and indeed, the only reason Geordie had begun to realize that all was not as it seemed was because there had been the occasional, very small glimpse that someone was working behind the scenes toward a determined goal. And once again, this seemed to point back to the spymaster.

In the end, there was little to be done; he was going nowhere without Etta, and he'd the strong sense that Etta was going nowhere without Marcello, who was obviously hip-deep in whatever plot was unfolding. He'd little choice but to trust the plan—whatever it was—and hope that the Romanies wouldn't take the first opportunity to shiv him in the back.

CHAPTER 33

Geordie found a likely clearing at the edge of a stand of trees, and quietly explained the logistics of the attack to the listening men—how far apart they'd set up; how to make certain the sticks were solidly planted in the dirt; how they would handle return fire from the fort, if there was any.

Staying low to the ground, Geordie then crept out into the middle of the clearing to gauge the distance to the Alcazar walls; he'd shorten the fuses so that the timing was right, based on what the women had told him. It was a shame that he couldn't test it out, first, but they could always adjust, depending on how it went. The Colonel used to say that even the most careful of plans should be scuttled in an instant, if things went awry, and that the side that was the nimblest in adjusting to catastrophe was the side that usually prevailed.

Geordie retreated back into the trees, and instructed the others, "The first group should return to the house, and make certain sure we can find this place in the dark—

leave a trail, if you have to. The second group will head out to find another launch site—Tornys, Minos and Gaston, come with me."

Once atop the opposite hill, Geordie duly chose another likely launching place—not exactly opposite the first one, for fear a stray rocket would cause more harm than good. As the men made their descent back down toward Santa Luisa, Minos and Tornys fell into step beside each other, which allowed Geordie to hang back a bit with Gaston. He'd been deprived of his chance to ask Gerard a few pertinent questions, but mayhap the man's brother knew a thing or two, and was willing to enlighten him.

To this end, Geordie began, "Your brother's gone, I hear. Do you know where?"

"No, *gadjo*."

Geordie had no idea whether this was true, but decided to accept what the other man said at face value. "Well, he's safe, and that's the main thing. Are you willing to answer a few questions?"

Gaston didn't look at him, and replied rather sullenly, "That depends on the question, *gadjo*."

Not necessarily encouraging, but Geordie hadn't much time, and so he began, "I think your brother was enlisted to counterfeit coins for Napoleon's people, along with Colonel Merryfield, who was to provide the raw silver. They were both working under threat, and so they'd little choice. But then something happened, and the Colonel wound up dead, whilst Gerard wound up under lock and key at the Alcazar."

The other man was silent for a few steps, and Geordie

continued, "I swear I'll not repeat what you tell me, friend. But if you know what happened, I'd be much obliged."

After a moment's consideration, Gaston replied, "The Colonel wanted my brother to sabotage Rochon—he said he'd pay him for it. He wanted Gerard to produce plates that appeared sound, but would not work properly, once they were put to use. By doing this, the counterfeiting operations would be delayed." He paused. "The British Colonel seemed to think that the delay was important— that Napoleon would not survive long, without the coins."

Geordie frowned, thinking this over. "Aye—it's a decent plan. And I suppose the Colonel hoped that—by the time the flaw was discovered—he and your brother would have had a chance to escape Rochon, since he'd have thought they were cooperating, all the while."

Gaston nodded. "Yes—I think so. But my brother had already suffered much at the hands of the Frenchman, and he was afraid. He feared the flaw might be discovered immediately—the plates were to be fashioned from a different metal than the usual."

This was of interest, and Geordie thought it over. "Zinc?" he wondered. "Or tin, mayhap; either will melt at high temperature—the Army tried to use tin for the rockets, and we discovered that flaw for ourselves. So; the idea was that the counterfeit plates would look legitimate, but they'd melt when the hot silver was poured into them, and thus no coins could be made."

Gaston nodded. "Yes. And the Colonel also had another plan—a surety, in the event it was discovered that the plates were flawed. He would sign a mortgage on the silver mines over to someone he could trust, someone who would go and claim them, so that the French could not use them."

"Me," Geordie said, a bit heavily. "I was supposed to be the surety."

Gaston nodded. "It was a good plan, but my brother told him no; Rochon had spies everywhere, and he was too afraid."

Lifting his brows, Geordie glanced over at him. "Oh? So, what happened?"

For the first time, Gaston smiled slightly. "The *Alkippa* happened, *gadjo*. The message she delivered could not have been more clear; my brother saw the Colonel's surety, riding the *Alkippa*, and he knew he had no choice."

Now; there's a stroke of luck, thought Geordie; *I'll never mock them about their magic horse again.*

Gaston continued, "So, my brother made the plates, and prepared the mortgage. But Rochon grew suspicious —it was taking longer than it should—and so the Colonel was killed, and Rochon's men seized Gerard. The Colonel's daughter had left for England with the plates, and they pursued her there, to seize them."

A bit grimly, Geordie asked, "What happened? Did they kill her?"

Gaston shrugged. "I know not."

Geordie let out a long breath. "I was supposed to rescue her. I should have obeyed orders."

Gaston looked up in surprise. "No, *gadjo*; the *Alkippa* wanted you here."

"I don't know as my mare is the best judge of things," Geordie replied.

But Gaston only shrugged. "You are not a *Rom*, and so you wouldn't understand."

Geordie nodded, and since they'd little time left, he offered baldly, "I wanted to broach another subject with you, friend. We're working with dangerous weapons, and I think you may be suffering from the drink."

As the stable building came into view, Gaston bent his head, studying the ground. "No more; my promise, *gadjo*. I have as little choice as my brother."

CHAPTER 34

As the sun began to set, the men settled in to the stables, to wait for midnight. The burlap sacks, containing their dangerous cargo, were piled in readiness, waiting to be transported up the hills. When it came time to eat dinner, Geordie was gratified to behold that it was Etta, smuggling-in the food instead of Ines. It seemed that his new bride was determined to yield no quarter to the other girl, and Geordie immediately decided that this fine show of possessiveness should be properly rewarded.

He rose, and walked over to approach her, after she'd doled out the food. "Mayhap you should take a brush to Jenny again, lass." Mainly, he wanted an excuse to duck out of sight with her; he shouldn't dally—not before a foray—but surely a few stolen kisses wouldn't be out of line.

Etta looked up to him in surprise. "Your mare is gone, Geordie."

With an oath, Geordie forgot about the kisses-plan and strode over to Jenny's stall. It was empty, and—with a mighty effort—he put a hand on the stall's partition and took hold of his temper. It only made sense, after all —the spymaster wouldn't know that Gerard's story about wanting the horse was a fish tale, and so the bribe had been delivered up as promised. Hopefully, they wouldn't load the mare on a ship bound for England; even his Jenny may have a tough time swimming the channel to come back to him. *I'll find her, one way or another,* he thought, a bit grimly. *I'll find her, and I'll find the Colonel's daughter, even if I have to scour England, top to bottom.*

"Where's Adao?" he asked abruptly. The lad also seemed to be missing.

"He is gone." This, said in the manner of one who realizes she might not be imparting welcome news.

Geordie cocked his head. "Do we know where?"

"The others may," she admitted. "But I do not."

Immediately, Geordie wheeled, and—with a few powerful strides—went over to confront the others, where they sat arrayed against the stable's wall. "Where's Adao?" he demanded.

The Romany men lifted their gazes to consider him, their expressions giving nothing away. Barely holding on to his temper, Geordie said, "All our plans will be for naught, if they catch the lad, and he's taken into the Alcazar."

Minos offered, "He won't be caught, *gadjo.*"

Geordie ran a hand down his face. "Here's the point, men. We need to have a command structure, so that I know you will do as I say, and not go off on your bloody own."

Gaston replied a bit sullenly, "We are not your soldiers, *gadjo*."

Geordie shook his head. "That doesn't matter, friend; the same thing applies to any group, working toward a goal. If everyone thinks they have a better idea, then we won't work together, and believe me, a unit that doesn't work together winds up dead."

Again, silence reigned, until Marcello offered, "I believe Adao went to monitor what will happen to your horse."

"I know the lad means well, but it's not a good idea," Geordie pronounced. "The spymaster's no fool, and if he thinks the lad's a spy, it won't go well for him." With a commander's glare, he ordered, "No one moves without my say-so, from here on out."

"Yes, *gadjo*," said Minos meekly.

Geordie was half-inclined to cuff him, but instead walked away, so as to cool his head. He didn't like this—didn't like the feeling that there were plots and counter-plots in play all around him. And—come to think of it—he wondered why the Romanies remained here, and hadn't melted away, like Adao. It didn't make sense, knowing what he now knew of the Romanies. They survived by guile, not by drawing attention to themselves.

He thought about this, a bit annoyed that it hasn't occurred to him before now. Marcello said he wanted vengeance for an injured kinsman—and Geordie was inclined to believe him—but Marcello wasn't a Romany, and that meant that the true Romanies didn't have a dog in this vengeance-fight. It made sense that Marcello would be working hand-in-glove with the British spymaster, since both men wanted the Alcazar taken down. And if the Padre were to be believed, the two men had an additional goal; they were looking to retrieve a treasure-casket from the Armory—something neither man had ever mentioned to Geordie.

But none of this explained why the Romanies were still here—still here, even after Gerard had been successfully rescued. Was the spymaster paying them? Possibly, but Geordie was fast coming to the conclusion that the Romanies wouldn't hesitate to double-cross the British spymaster. Not only that, but it seemed to him that neither tribe much cared about what happened to the other. So; why were they still here, working together, and willing to risk their lives so as to help the spymaster destroy the Alcazar? Again, it seemed a bit ominous to him; there was an element at play, here, that he didn't understand, and he sincerely hoped he wasn't left to be the scapegoat, when the smoke cleared away.

Meanwhile, he'd a new bride to kiss, and so he pushed these troubling thoughts aside, and motioned to Etta. "I'll escort you back to the house, if I may."

"You may," Etta agreed in a demure tone, although the dimple appeared in her cheek.

When they came alongside the smokehouse, he pulled her into the doorway alcove and gathered her to him—Lord, but she felt good; soft in all the right places, and exactly the right height, for her arms to fit under his. She lifted her face, and he kissed her—gently, being as he didn't want to startle her overmuch—and before he could get lost in the sensation—which would be mighty easy to do—he reluctantly pulled away.

"Mrs. Venables," he declared, as he held her close, and rested his cheek alongside her temple. "I'm counting the minutes until I have more than a few snatches of time alone with you."

"I, too, Geordie," she whispered, and lifted on tiptoe to insist he kiss her again.

Nothing loath, he did—a deeper kiss, this time—so that she was a bit breathless, when he regretfully withdrew. "I can't dally with you, lass—more's the pity— and I won't ask you to betray your brother, but damned if a lot of things aren't adding up."

She pulled away to look into his face with alarm. "Do you think you are in danger?"

"Nothing that I can't handle," he assured her. "But I don't like the fact that Adao has gone off somewhere without telling me. And speaking of such, where is Ines?"

"She has gone over to the Alcazar, to listen and report back."

He nodded, and was reminded of his earlier observations. "Is it possible she's a Romany, too?"

Surprised, Etta shook her head. "No—at least, I do not believe so."

Rather than alarm her further, he bent to kiss her quickly, and asked in a light tone, "And what are you, lass? You've a fistful of names."

Her eyes shining, she replied, "I am Mrs. Venables."

Since this answer deserved another kiss, Geordie didn't hesitate, and even made so bold as to explore her body a bit, since the lass did seem a bit frustrated that he wasn't doing his duty by her.

"Forgive me, for interrupting."

Geordie looked up to see Marcello, approaching from the stables. He could tell by the man's posture that he wasn't bringing good news, and so Geordie straightened up to face him. "Let's hear it, then."

"We may have to move the attack forward. We have news that Rochon has seized the Padre."

Geordie's brows drew together. "Has he? Bloody *hell*. Who made the report?"

"Ines."

"Can we believe what she tells us?"

"I believe we can, Captain."

Geordie's mouth formed a grim line. "Then we should clear out, on the double. I can't imagine the Padre would hold up well under torture."

"As you say," Marcello agreed.

As Etta hurried back into the house, the two men strode over to the stables, and Geordie called the others together. "We've a problem; the Padre's been seized, which makes me think this Rochon fellow must be suspicious that there's a plan afoot—and if he's discovered that the wine casks contain black powder, then he'll know it for sure. "We need to pack up, quick-like, and move the rockets—"

"Shouldn't we attack immediately?" Marcello interrupted.

Geordie looked over at him in surprise. "Nay; first, we've got to extract the Padre."

Silently, everyone stared at him.

With a furious scowl, Geordie insisted, "We leave no man behind."

Minos pointed out, "We are not soldiers, *gadjo*, and the Padre is not one of ours."

"I'll pretend I didn't hear that," Geordie replied in an ominous tone. "I'll go in to get him; I'll tell them the British Army wants to ask him a few questions, because we're worried he's spying for the French. They don't dare call my bluff, even if they know it's a fish tale. Meanwhile, we have to find a place to hide the rockets, quick-like."

Minos spoke up again. "There is a cellar in the smokehouse, *gadjo*. A hidden storage place, beneath a trap door."

"Aye, then," Geordie nodded, and wondered why no one had mentioned this to him, before. "Let's move them down quickly—careful, everyone, no flames, and don't let them get damp—and then clear out until I come back with the Padre. I don't doubt you lot know how to hide out in the woods until I get back. When it's clear, I'll leave my hat on the pump handle. Everybody got it?"

The others nodded, and Geordie had to hope that they would do as they were told—a faint hope, with this group, but he'd little other choice. And to add insult to injury, he'd no horse, and thus would present a strange figure, having to brave the Alcazar on foot.

Yanking down the brim of his hat, he set out.

CHAPTER 35

"I'm here on official business," Geordie announced, as he showed the guard at the gate his worn and much-folded Army passage papers. "We think there's a French spy within, and I'm to transport him to Talavera, so that my commanding officer can question him."

The Spanish soldier squinted at the English document, and nodded. "If you will wait here, *señor.*"

"Captain," Geordie corrected, in an arrogant manner.

"*Si*, Captain," the man agreed, and hurried off.

In short order, the man returned and indicated Geordie was to follow him. 'The Comandante will see you, Captain."

"Of course, he will," said Geordie curtly. "This is a very serious matter, and if the Comandante is housing a French spy, there will be hell to pay."

He followed the escort to the Comandante's offices, and entered to see that there were two men awaiting him, the Comandante and another man, who was dressed in civilian clothes, and wearing an arm-sling.

"Sir," said Geordie, with a curt nod. "I am here to escort a prisoner back to the British installation at Talavera. He is posing as a Spanish priest, and we believe he is directly responsible for the peace-time deaths of British soldiers."

The Comandante glanced at the other man for direction, and Geordie deduced that this must be the Rochon fellow that everyone was so afraid of—which made sense, if he'd been shot in the shoulder, lately. It was rather surprising, though, as he was an ordinary-appearing fellow, and not fearsome in the least.

Rochon asked in a mild tone "Why do you believe the priest is a French spy, Captain?"

"That is none of your business, friend," said Geordie curtly. "Hand him over, now."

Rochon spread his hands. "I confess I would be more inclined to believe your story if we did not already know that the man is a spy for the British."

The Comandante interrupted to plead, "Please, *señor*; I had no idea—"

Without looking at him, Rochon said in the same mild tone, "You will be quiet, if you please."

Swiftly, Geordie changed his tactics, and cursed himself for a fool; it was completely plausible that the Padre was a spy for the British, and this should have occurred to him long before now. The man was well-placed to hear what was going on in the area, not to mention that he visited the Alcazar often, to drink with the fort's commander. Geordie had assumed it was

Marcello, who'd been keeping the British spymaster informed, but mayhap it was the Padre. Or both—no one was who they seemed, in this fantastic tale.

With a show of reluctance, Geordie bowed his head in acknowledgement, but his voice held a measure of steel. "Be that as it may, all the more reason why I will take him with me, and nothing more need be said on the subject."

It was a gamble, but he was counting on the fact that —no matter what was afoot, here—they dared not antagonize the British, who currently held the whip hand in Spain.

"Of course," said Rochon immediately, in a placating manner. "Many apologies, Captain. Come; we will fetch him straightaway, and you may see for yourself that he has come to no harm."

He called for an escort, and as the guard entered the office, he immediately paused on the threshold. "You!" the man exclaimed, staring at Geordie in disbelief.

"Why, hallo again," Geordie said to the man who'd knocked his tooth out. "I've been looking for you."

The guard clenched his fists, but Rochon raised a hand in warning. "Hold, please. We will treat our visitor kindly."

"You will, indeed," Geordie returned. "Else I've a friend with grey eyes who will rain down hellfire upon your head." A shame, that he didn't know the spymaster's name, but hopefully the allusion was sufficient.

The bluff seemed to turn the trick, since a calculating expression flashed across the Frenchman's face. *He's not sure I'm telling the truth*, thought Geordie, *but he wonders if he shouldn't take the chance—the reference to the grey eyes seems to have given him pause.*

"Come," Rochon continued in a placating manner. "You may retrieve the prisoner, and I hope you will accept my apologies for this little misunderstanding."

Geordie nodded curtly, and with a show of casual bravado, strode across the graveled yard with the Comandante and Rochon, although he was made uneasy by the fact that the brutal guard seemed to have been given a signal to accompany them. *Rochon's still not sure whether he should simply seize me,* Geordie thought; *and throw me in with the Padre. Here's hoping I can bluff my way out of here with a whole skin.*

They walked past the Armory, and approached the service area of the main facility—the kitchens, it looked to be, and Rochon turned his head to say to Geordie. "The priest is being held in the cellars, here."

"Then bring him up," said Geordie, coming to a halt in the yard. "I'm not such a fool that I'll go below ground."

"No, no—of course," Rochon replied, and then issued instructions to the posted sentry to go retrieve the prisoner.

Geordie took the opportunity to remark to the guard, "I've a gift, I've been meaning to give to you."

But the man would not be baited, and stood like a statue, without meeting Geordie's eyes.

The Padre emerged from the narrow steps, blinking against the light of the sentry's lantern, and holding up an arm to shade his eyes against the setting sun. He'd a black eye, but other than that, he didn't seem much the worse for wear.

"What's to do?" The older man asked in a querulous voice. "You can't treat a man of God in such a way. Wait until my Bishop hears of this—he'll excommunicate the lot of you."

"Quiet," Geordie ordered. "You are coming with me."

The priest frowned, as he considered the Scotsman. "Am I?"

Geordie jerked his head. "Let's go."

Geordie turned with all confidence, but he sensed that it still hung in the balance, whether he'd actually be allowed to leave with the Padre, and it was at this juncture that they beheld Ines hurrying toward them, and wiping her hands on her apron.

"*Señor*," she called out to the Comandante. "*Señor*—a word."

"Away, girl," said Rochon impatiently.

"A moment, *señor*," the Comandante explained to the Frenchman in an earnest tone. "This girl has been helpful to me, in the past." He lowered his voice and said with some innuendo, "She hears much."

Oh-oh, thought Geordie, but then immediately decided to withhold his judgment; if Ines had wanted to betray them, she'd had plenty of opportunity before now. More likely she was attempting to come to his aid; he'd stay alert for a signal, and see what she had to say.

The Comandante asked, "What is it, Ines? Quickly."

Glancing with some nervousness at Rochon, Ines offered in an uncharacteristically hesitant voice, "I—I am sorry to interrupt, *señor*, but I thought you should be made aware. The Gypsy Queen is at the gate. She demands to see you, but the guards have turned her away."

No, thought Geordie in deep dismay; *no, no, no, lass.* Lord alive, if Etta was trying to come within, it would make an escape that much more complicated.

The Comandante frowned. "How does this concern me? What does she want?"

"She wishes to be paid, *señor*. She seeks reparations."

Impatiently, the Comandante waved her away. "What nonsense; there's nothing to be done. Tell them to send her on her way, Ines."

Ines lowered her voice, and glanced meaningfully toward Geordie. "I ran to tell you, *señor*, that she speaks of the British—she says they cheated her of her reward."

There was a small silence, as Rochon gazed thoughtfully at Geordie. "Does she, *vraiment*? Then by all means—let us hear what she has to say."

CHAPTER 36

Whilst Ines hurried away, Rochon turned to address Geordie, his eyes narrowed. "What role did the British play, in the murder of my prisoner?"

"You speak in tongues," Geordie scoffed. "You should stay out of the sun."

"You will tell me, and sooner rather than later," Rochon insisted, his voice carrying a veiled threat.

Geordie cocked a skeptical brow at him. "I'm mighty surprised that the likes of you are threatening the likes of me. And I'm mighty surprised to hear that you are holding a prisoner, here. I would have guessed you were French, myself."

Before Rochon could respond to this heavy-handed reminder that he held no legal authority, the Padre interrupted them to whine, "As for me, I have been much abused, and I would greatly appreciate a drink of water."

"Quiet," snapped the Comandante. "You have caused me trouble enough, old man."

"There's more trouble to come," Geordie said to the Comandante in a menacing tone. "We've caught wind of some very disturbing information about your activities, here."

Whilst the Comandante stared at him in acute distress, Geordie cast a severe glance at the Padre. "You; follow me," he commanded. With any luck, he could bluster his way out of here, and turn Etta around before she came in at the gate.

But this strategy was not to be successful, as Rochon held up a hand. "Hold a minute, Captain; we will hear what the gypsy girl has to say, before we decide who has broken the peace treaty."

Geordie shrugged impatiently. "Suit yourself." There seemed little point to arguing; he wanted to appear confident, and he could see that the Frenchman was weighing his options, trying to decide if Geordie was bluffing, and whether he should just seize them all, and sort it out later. Taking a swift, covert assessment of the personnel in the area between them and the gate, Geordie didn't like the odds; what was the lass thinking, to come into the lion's den?

They waited in the graveled yard as Etta came into view—very regal, and riding Jenny, of all things. Which truly wasn't much of a surprise—the mare must have escaped to come back to him, yet again—or more likely, escaped with Adao's contrivance; the boy wasn't going to sit idly by, and let the magic horse sail away to England.

In fact, it was more of a surprise that Etta had come in alone, bold as brass, and with a face like a thundercloud.

It seemed very unlike her, to do such a thing, and it also seemed clear she hadn't consulted with her brother, in taking such a risk. Lord love the lass, for trying to come to his aid, but she was complicating things mightily.

As she came closer, the Comandante exclaimed, "Why; that's the horse—the horse the brother stole, after he killed the prisoner. This girl must know where her brother is."

"Good. Then we shall find out, too," said Rochon, in an unpleasant tone.

Behind a stoic expression, Geordie hid his dismay; *lass, lass, you didn't think this through—these people are ruthless.*

Etta halted Jenny before them, and announced imperiously, "I have been cheated, and I demand to be paid."

Geordie blinked, since this didn't sound at all like the Etta he knew. Full of brass, she was.

Rochon stepped forward to put a hand on Jenny's bridle, and gaze up at her. "Where is your brother? He is wanted for murder."

Etta tossed her head. "He went to the British, and received his reward." Pointing an imperative finger at the Comandante, she continued hotly, "But no one remembers me; no one gives me *my* reward, and my brother refuses to share. So, I took his horse." Her eyes narrowed. "You will pay me, or I will make you very, very sorry. I will curse you, and everyone in your family."

Rochon's sharp gaze rested on the other man. "What do you know of this?"

"Nothing," the Comandante insisted, taken aback. "*Madre de Dios*, I have no idea what she is talking about, I swear—"

But it seemed Rochon was entertaining an unwelcome suspicion, and abruptly, he asked the Comandante, "Is it possible that the prisoner yet lives? That the British paid these people to stage a rescue?"

"No—no, no—I can assure you—" Aghast, the man implored, "*Madre Santísima*, you must believe me; indeed, I saw him die with my own eyes."

Incredulous, Etta stared at Rochon as though he were an unpleasant insect, beneath her feet. "Are you a *fool*? Do you not listen? It is *my* bridegroom who was killed, and my brother cheated me of my reward." To emphasize this point, she thrust a finger at him, her face aflame. "I demand payment; I have been cheated."

Rochon tilted his head in a manner that indicated Geordie. "Was this the man who paid your brother?"

"Lord alive, but you spout nonsense," Geordie scoffed, and wondered if this was the correct tack to take.

With a stormy expression, Etta glanced at Geordie with impatience. "No; the British paid my brother at the tavern—the one in San Pablo." She lowered her voice, and added with a great deal of meaning, "The meeting place."

There was a small, profound silence. The tavern was the gambling-den where the Colonel had been killed— and where Geordie had got beat-up, for asking too many questions. It seemed to Geordie that the atmosphere changed, suddenly, and that it was Rochon, now, who was taken aback. No doubt the man was worried that—if what the girl was saying was true—the British had infiltrated his organization, and knew whatever it was that he was plotting, there.

Coming to a decision, Rochon indicated the cellar steps before them, and said in a deceptively courteous tone, "If you will come within, girl; I will pay you handsomely for whatever you will tell me."

But Etta only tossed her head, defiant. "I am not such a fool. Pay me now for what I am owed, and then I will think it over."

With an inward qualm, Geordie noted that Rochon glanced in an unspoken message toward his henchman. His voice now containing a hint of steel, the Frenchman continued, "Come, come; we mustn't argue. One way or the other, you will tell me everything you know."

Whilst Geordie gathered himself to make a move—no matter what, he couldn't let them take Etta down the stairs—she retorted angrily, "I know there is a delta of two."

With some confusion, Rochon frowned at her. "*Que?*"

Geordie blinked. *A delta of two? For the holy love of Christ, a fuse had been lit. What fuse? No matter—it was time for action, which was just as well; he was mighty tired of play-acting.*

Without warning, he turned to land a mighty blow on the guard's chin, before whirling to attack Rochon before he could draw his weapon. It wasn't necessary, though; the Padre had used the distraction to leap atop Rochon, viciously wrenching his wounded shoulder as the man collapsed to the ground, crying out in acute pain.

Aghast, the Comandante attempted to pull the little

priest from the Frenchman, which gave Geordie the opportunity to bring down the butt of his pistol on the back of the Spanish officer's head, so that the man collapsed beside the agonized Rochon.

Quickly, Geordie pulled the fallen men's pistols, and then glanced up at the soldiers who'd raised their weapons in surprise, and were advancing toward them. "Stay back," he shouted in Spanish. "This is a British operation, and the Third Division waits outside the walls. Anyone who opens fire will be fired upon."

Uncertain, the soldiers hesitated, and the Padre urged Geordie in a low voice, "Go—go with the girl; I'll hold a gun to the Comandante's head, and keep them back."

"You're a brave man," said Geordie gravely, and then quickly felled the Padre with another swift uppercut to the jaw. Heaving the collapsing priest to his shoulder, Geordie strode toward Etta. "Quickly," he said, as he flung the priest up before her, on Jenny's withers. "Hold on to him, and stay close. I'll bring the Comandante with me as a hostage, and we'll brazen our way out the back gate. Here we go."

"No, we won't, Geordie," she replied calmly, as she helped him with the fallen priest.

Geordie looked up to her in surprise. "No?"

"We must not go that way."

Her reasons became clear almost immediately, as a huge explosion rent the air, nearly staggering Geordie off his feet.

Etta leaned forward to cover the priest, and Geordie threw his arms over both of them as best he could, as falling bits of brick and other debris rained down around them. Looking up, he saw thick, black smoke billowing out from the Armory, the dark plumes quickly obscuring much of the yard. With cries of alarm, some of the soldiers began to race toward the burning building, but Geordie shouted in Spanish, "Stay back; stay back—it is dangerous."

His warning was proved true, as yet another explosion rent the air, followed closely by another and another, as heavy clouds of smoke swirled around the inferno of flames that engulfed what was left of the Armory.

Geordie turned to his mare, who stood—as she'd stood in many a battlefield—patiently awaiting orders. "Clear out," he ordered, pulling her toward the front gate. "Let's go."

"In a moment," Etta called out, as the mare began to dance beneath her restraining hand, and to Geordie's astonishment, she drew down a small pistol, and aimed it squarely at Rochon, as the Frenchman continued to moan in helpless agony on the ground.

"Nay, lass," Geordie said, and stepped before the barrel of the pistol. "I'll not be a party to this. You said your kinsman's not dead, but wounded, and now this one's sore-wounded. An eye for an eye; no more, and no less."

She met his eyes, and considered this. "As you say, Geordie," she reluctantly agreed, and lowered her weapon.

They hadn't time to further discuss the matter, however, because Geordie suddenly heard a familiar whistling sound, overhead. "Christ Almighty!" he shouted; "They're firing off the rockets!"

"Yes," Etta called back, unsurprised, as she gathered the Padre's coat tightly in her hands. "We should run to the front gate, now."

Keeping his head down, Geordie raced beside Jenny as she loped toward the gate, and hoped the guards had left their posts, in the confusion of the attack.

No such luck; a soldier approached them with his rifle at the ready, and Geordie tried to decide how best to battle his way through the gate, hampered by his two companions; he was reluctant to shoot the guard, but given the circumstances, he'd no real choice. "Stay behind me," he shouted to Etta, and drew his weapon.

But he was yet again to be surprised, as she called out in an urgent tone, "Do not shoot—it is Marcello."

Blinking, Geordie realized that this was indeed the case, as the other man blocked their way, in a mock-menacing manner.

"Throw down your weapon," Geordie ordered, pretending to draw down on the man. "And open the gate. Quickly, man."

"In a moment," Marcello replied, as he continued to

hold them at musket-point.

What are we waiting for? Geordie thought, as more rockets whistled over their heads, landing a bit wildly as the soldiers within the fort shouted warnings to each other, and ran to take cover. "Stay out of the buildings," Geordie turned to shout at them in Spanish. "Keep to the perimeter." With some relief, he saw several soldiers relay his warning, as more rockets streaked through the sky, making huge explosions wherever they landed, and adding to the general pandemonium.

The scene was to become even more chaotic, as a group of panicked servants suddenly came streaming out the main building's service porch, running pell-mell toward them at the gate, with the women shrieking and the men urging them along.

"Open the gates!" a man demanded, and then—as though to emphasize the point—an explosion rent through the building that the servants had just exited, flames and smoke suddenly billowing from the windows.

Interesting; I didn't see a rocket land in that area, Geordie thought, as Marcello retreated to pull on the chain that opened the gates. *Someone's planted some bombs, it seems, but I'll not be hanging around to confirm this.*

As he pulled Jenny along with the crowd that streamed through the gate, Geordie saw that Ines was amongst the frightened servants, covered in soot and nearly stumbling, as she cradled a heavy bundle before her—a child? He fought against the crowd so as to go over and help her, but then he saw that she abandoned the bundle at Marcello's feet, and quickly fled through the gate, along with all the others.

With dawning comprehension, Geordie's thoughts turned a bit grim, as he mingled with the fleeing servants to lead his horse out into the meadow—he'd no real fear of being fired upon, since the Spanish soldiers would be loath to fire on their neighbors. *For the holy and merciful love of Christ; it's always been about the damned treasure-casket,* he realized, as he split off from the crowd, and quickly made for the cover of the tree-line. *And I'm a right fool, for letting myself get distracted by these so-called revenge plots, which were nothing more than a cover for this operation. The British spymaster couldn't show that he was behind all this, but now he's not only got his counterfeiter back, he's got his treasure-casket, too—the one that no one is supposed to know about.*

When they made the cover of the trees, Geordie paused to catch his breath, and assess their position. "How's the Padre?"

"He's regaining his wits, I think," Etta responded.

Geordie pulled the priest off the horse, and then steadied him against her shoulder as the other man moaned and blinked. "Where's Marcello?" he asked Etta. He may as well ask; the lass certainly seemed to know more about these events than he did. "Should we try to find him?"

"No; instead, we must cross the river," Etta explained. "There is a safe house, on the other side."

In a grim tone, Geordie replied, "I'll not walk into any more ambushes, Etta."

"I am so sorry," she said softly, and reached down to touch his shoulder. "But I could not tell you—not without jeopardizing everyone else."

"No more o' that," he replied, a bit sternly. "I may not have the ordering of you, but you're to be honest with me, lass."

"You ordered me not to shoot the Frenchman," she pointed out. "And I truly, truly wanted to."

"Aye; there's that," he acknowledged fairly.

"Forgive me, Geordie."

He lifted his gaze to hers, a grave concern raised within his breast, based on the events of the past half-hour. "Are we wed? In truth?"

She smiled. "We are. If you will still have me."

"Fah; I wouldn't take him—he's *un hijo de perra*," pronounced the Padre, as he eyed Geordie sourly, and gingerly explored his chin. "Caught me off guard—you will never do it again, *señor*."

"So, you say," said Geordie mildly.

The priest had taken off his hat to rub his head, and before he could come up with a suitable retort, he paused. "Will you look at that?" he said, with some satisfaction.

Geordie turned to see that a red glow hovered in the darkening sky, as the whole of the Alcazar was now engulfed in flames. He nodded. "They'll be busy, so we should move on, before they've had a chance to regroup."

"The river," Etta said again. "There will be fishing boats, waiting to take us across."

Geordie weighed his options, and decided he'd best comply; he was fast-coming to the conclusion that there was a well-planned-out scheme unfolding, and that his own part seemed to be mostly extraneous. Besides, he should probably as the lass asked—she seemed handy with a pistol.

He nodded in concession. "Let's go, then." He asked the Padre, "Should we put you up behind Etta?"

But the disgruntled priest shook him off. "Fah; I'm perfectly capable, *Ingles*."

"Not *Ingles*—*Escosés*," Geordie corrected.

The priest made a sound of impatience. "*Madre de Dios* —why does it matter?"

But Geordie only replied in a tone that brooked no argument, "It matters a lot. I'm a Scotsman, no more, and no less."

"All right, all right; no need to be so touchy." The priest glanced around. "We mustn't tarry. Where's the boy?"

"What boy?" asked Geordie, suddenly alert.

"Here," said Adao, as he stepped forward from the shelter of a tree.

"There's not a soul in this place who knows how to obey orders," Geordie observed grimly.

"Come; I will lead you to the river," urged Adao, as he gestured for them to follow.

Stubbornly, Geordie declared, "I'm going nowhere without my horse."

"I will swim her across, *gadjo*," Adao offered. "She is a strong swimmer."

Geordie considered this for a moment, but decided he'd little choice in the matter. That, and Jenny looked as though she was half-asleep, which usually meant there was no danger to be had. "All right, lad. Stay in sight, and for the holy love of Christ, don't let anyone steal her."

Adao flashed a grin, and then turned to lead them through the trees.

CHAPTER 38

They were rowed across the broad River Tagus by men who made little comment, and kept their lanterns shuttered, so that they were guided mainly by the moonlight.

Geordie sat next to Etta in the stern of the dory, with an arm around her against the river breeze—she wore her gypsy blouse, and hadn't a shawl. She'd moved an arm across her lap to hold his fingers in hers, and he silently kissed her temple, thinking, *I understand, lass; you're sorry you couldn't let me know what was planned, but it was too important to take the risk.* He forgave her, of course—and who was to say it wasn't the proper course to take; after all, he wasn't one for pretenses.

Sound tended to carry across the water, and so he stayed silent, and kept his questions to himself, for the time being. Besides, he'd the feeling that he may as well be whistling in the wind, if he was hoping to finally get a straight answer.

Whilst the oars dipped quietly in the river, he listened

for sounds of pursuit, but didn't hear any. He also listened for sounds of a horse, swimming with a lad on her back, but didn't hear that, either—no doubt Adao was choosing his own path; the boy seemed well-versed in evading the enemy, and since he'd been reared with *guerrillas*, this only made sense.

All in all, he was content to be led wherever Etta wished him to go—a novel experience, for someone who'd taken the lead for most of his life—but he felt it was the right tack to take, in this instance. He'd been roundly hoodwinked, but he didn't have the sense there was any animosity behind it. Instead, it must be as he'd surmised; there was a British plan to rescue Gerard—as well as retrieve the casket—but that plan relied on the counterfeiter's willingness to cooperate. And Gerard's cooperation had—amazingly enough—rested on Geordie's horse.

The *Alkippa* had suddenly shown up in the Romany man's orbit, and her presence overrode even the promises of freedom and riches by the British—such was the strength of Gerard's belief. Indeed, Geordie had heard tales of similar doings, during the Indian wars in America —that the British had to be careful not to run afoul of native superstitions, in recruiting their allies. And so, Adao had been dispatched to steal his mare, but Jenny— true to form—had refused to remain stolen, and so Geordie was reluctantly incorporated into their plan.

Geordie frowned, because—even though this was a plausible theory—it ran against a hurdle that didn't make a lot of sense. Geordie was almost certain that the spymaster, himself, had also been roundly hoodwinked.

Gerard had certainly lied to the man about wanting to be King of the Gypsies, and it also seemed he'd never told the spymaster about the mortgage, and about Colonel Merryfield's plan.

There must be a reason for all this, and although Geordie always had the impression that someone very clever was behind this operation, he was fast-coming to the conclusion that the person in command wasn't necessarily the spymaster.

As the opposite shore materialized in the darkness, he decided he'd just have to be patient; there were pieces missing from this puzzle, still—not to mention that it all seemed far too complicated, for his poor soldier's brain. The only thing that seemed certain was the fact that he'd been drawn-in—implausibly—because of his bonny black mare. It would be almost amusing, were it not for the fact that he hadn't much liked playing blind man's bluff, and he hadn't much liked the idea that he might meet the same fate as the Colonel. To the good, he'd gained a fine wife, for his troubles—that she was as handy with a pistol as she was with a fishing-line seemed almost too good to be true.

Once they landed, they were silently escorted inland until they came to a large farmhouse, and then—after waiting for an "all clear" bird call—they quietly filed into the house via the kitchen door. Geordie took the opportunity to murmur to Marcello, "I'll be staying with my wife, brother." He'd decided that this would be an excellent test to confirm that he and Etta were truly married.

"Of course," Marcello readily agreed. "But be aware

there is a hidden room beneath the floor of the pantry, in the event the enemy musters up a search. We will have plenty of warning, if we need to retreat there."

Geordie nodded. "A lot of these houses have hidden rooms, it seems."

"Yes—there was an active *guerrilla* network in this area, during the war, and I suppose that explains it."

"Aye," said Geordie thoughtfully.

A maid servant offered to escort Etta upstairs, and Geordie recognized her as Sasha, the woman from the gypsy caravan, although no explanation was given as to how she'd managed to return to this area, or where she'd been. As Etta followed Sasha up the stairs, Geordie watched his wife's retreating figure, and decided it was a mortal shame that the lass would probably never have the opportunity to wear gypsy garb, again.

Marcello interrupted his thoughts to explain, "A cold supper has been laid out on the kitchen work-table. There are scouts posted who will alert us, if there is a need to retreat, but we do not expect a search tonight."

"Nay," Geordie agreed. Unlikely that Rochon was in any shape to give orders, and presumably, the soldiers at the fort would be more interested in putting out the fire, than trying to chase gypsies around at night.

As they headed toward the table, the back door opened a crack, and Geordie was gratified to see Adao leaning in, and soaked to the skin. "*Gadjo*," he greeted Geordie with a grin.

"Good lad," said Geordie. "How did she do?"

"I will rub her down, but I wanted to tell you we made it safely, and that she swam well."

Geordie nodded, and decided not to mention he knew this already, since the mare had managed to swim him across the River Zadorra at Vitoria, where so many others —men and horses—had died. "Thank you, laddie; I'm ready to take a dip in the river, myself."

"If you are willing to wait, you may bathe after Etta," Marcello suggested. "There is but one tub."

"Willingly," Geordie agreed, and then moved over to join the Padre at the kitchen work-table, where the priest was helping himself.

"I have been ill-used," the Padre groused. "My poor head hurts, and I am tired of cold meats."

"It's a shame we've no beefsteak," Geordie noted. "We could lay it across your black eye."

The Padre gave him a withering look. "You mock me, but the Comandante had an excellent side of beef, hanging in the curing room, and now it is up in flames."

With a firm hand on the other's back, Geordie instructed, "Come along; take your sorry excuse for a meal, and eat it out on the stoop with me. I want to make sure there are no hard feelings, from knocking you about."

The Padre sighed heavily. "I am called to forgive," he replied with resignation, and allowed Geordie to steer him out the back door.

After taking a careful look 'round in the darkness, Geordie settled on the stoop with the Padre, and then bit into his bread-and-ham with gusto—he was mighty hungry, after such a long day. "What do you think will happen to the Comandante? Will he hang?"

The Padre paused in surprise. "Why would he? It was not his fault, that a Romany tribe killed his prisoner, and then the other tribe took its revenge."

Geordie chewed, and tilted his head. "No—I was referring to your operation. If the Comandante wasn't a participant in your plan, it's hard to believe that someone who rose to the level of Comandante could be so dense."

Lifting a corner of his mouth, the older man replied, "You are unfamiliar with the *Afrancesado* officers, *señor*. I can assure you that many of them are very, very dense."

Geordie chuckled, and glanced over at the other man. "I fouled everything up, when I went in to extract you."

"You speak nonsense, *señor*," the Padre replied, as he

tore off another piece of bread. "It is you, who should stay out of the sun."

Smiling, Geordie re-addressed his own meal. "You allowed yourself to be captured, so as to be on-site during the rocket attack. I think you were assigned to grab this treasure-casket, once the Armory walls were breached—the Armory is very near the prisoner's cells. Your people may have even dug-out a secret access to the Armory ahead of time, so as to be certain you could get to it."

"A fairy tale," scoffed the priest, who continued to eat.

"And then I showed up, to rescue you when you didn't want rescuing."

The Padre made a derisive noise, as he paused to take a swig from the flask, and then slowly wipe his mouth with his sleeve. "Fah; charging in like a blind bull, you were. As if I needed rescuing, like a helpless puppy."

Geordie shrugged. "How was I to know it was all part of the plan? That's why Marcello didn't want a lethal attack—you were going to be on site, seizing the casket, in all the confusion."

The older man shook his head in wonder. "How could we have known you'd insist on charging in, alone?"

"If any man-jack of you had served under Colonel Merryfield, you'd have known," Geordie advised him sternly. "The Fightin' Third leaves no man behind."

The Padre heaved a mighty sigh. "*Madre de Dios*, but you are a stubborn man."

"It has stood me in good stead, all in all, with this time being no exception."

They ate in silence, until Geordie thought he heard a rustling sound, in the darkness. With a hand on his pistol, he peered out toward the trees to see the figure of a woman, emerging from the darkness—barely discernable in the moonlight—and as she approached, he realized it was Ines.

"Lass," he greeted her. "I'm that glad you made it out with a whole skin."

She'd been cleaned up since he'd seen her at the gate —her face was no longer streaked with soot—but he duly noted that one of her hands was bandaged.

"And I am glad to see you, Captain." She reached within her bosom in a provocative manner, but to the Padre's palpable disappointment, she only drew out an oilcloth packet, sewn up around the edges. "The Senora sends you your marriage lines, Captain. She thought to sew the parchment in an oilskin, so as to keep it from getting wetted."

Geordie nodded his thanks as he casually accepted the packet, and thought it a clever way to deliver his mortgage along with his marriage lines, with no one the wiser. "Your mistress is a right one—a lot like you, lass."

"You are kind, Captain." With a lingering smile, she continued into the kitchen.

"Now, there's a steady lass," Geordie offered into the silence. "Brave, and able."

"*Si,*" said the Padre, and for once, he sounded completely sincere.

Geordie glanced at him. "So; all's well that ends well? The spymaster's got his treasure? I feel as though I've a vested interest, and it seems only fair that I find out, considering the pains I had to take."

The older man gazed out into the dark night, and

shook his head sadly. "Ah, *señor*; that poor man is sore-disappointed, I hear. It seems the casket was filled with rocks, instead of with royal treasure."

Geordie raised his brows. "Is that so?"

The Padre stretched out his legs, and offered in all sorrow, "No doubt it was looted long ago. Indeed, it was a fond hope, to believe that such a treasure remained undisturbed, over all these years."

Geordie eyed him, sidelong. "A shame, that the English won't lay their hands on the Spanish royal treasure."

The other man nodded solemnly. "*Si.* I must offer the spymaster some of my fine wine, so that we can together bemoan this terrible turn of events."

Smiling, Geordie brushed off his lap and rose to his feet. "You're a right gafty one, if I might say so."

The Padre shrugged, and then repeated Geordie's own words back to him. "I am a Spaniard, *señor*; nothing more, and nothing less."

CHAPTER 40

I've got to try to be patient, Geordie sternly warned himself. *I can't go pawing at the lass, and scare her silly.* Being as he'd never taken a wife to bed before, he could be forgiven for being a bit uncertain as to how to go about it. Not to mention that she was some sort of nob, and therefore unused to hulking, rough fellows like himself. *Easy does it,* he cautioned; *best to start out slow.* This, of course, would be a novel approach, considering his recent experiences in this department— war tended to curtail a man's time and choices.

He was immersed in a tub of hot water—cooling off, now—and thoroughly enjoying the sensation; he hadn't been in a tub in a long, long time. Not that he'd make it a habit—he was one who favored hard living over soft; it was bred into his bones.

The door opened and—to his surprise—Ines slipped in, bearing a towel. "Careful," he warned her bluntly. "I've a new bride, and she knows how to handle a pistol."

The serving girl laughed, and then stood at her ease next to the tub—close enough so that he could see that her eyebrows were a bit singed. "I've only come to say goodbye, Captain."

"Where will you go, lass?"

She raised her brows. "I will return to the Senora's house, of course."

Idly, he lifted a hand to play with the water. "I only ask, because if I were taking a guess—and it's only a guess—I'd guess that you know what's happened to this royal treasure, that was switched-out for a pile o' rocks. But damned if I know who you're working for. Not the British, it seems."

Her eyes opened wide, Ines disclaimed, "Why, I don't know what you mean, Captain."

He shrugged. "Dinna fash yourself, lass; I reckon it's not my business. As long as it doesn't wind up in Napoleon's coffers, it matters naught to me."

With a smile, the girl leaned down to caress the side of his face, and whisper near his ear, "No, Captain; instead, it will go back to where it belongs—resting beneath a fruit tree, to await the end of these endless wars." Her eyes met his in invitation. "Perhaps you will come to visit it with me, and we will taste the fruit, together."

He chuckled. "I appreciate the thought, lass, but I'm a married man, now."

She shrugged slightly, and straightened up so as to fold the towel over a chairback. "The invitation stands, Captain. *Vaya con Dios*."

"*Vaya con Dios*," he replied, and watched as she

slipped out the door. *Another doughty lass*, he thought; *just like my Etta. I've met more than a few, during this cursed war.*

Hard on this thought, Etta herself came through the door, carrying another towel, and looking a little self-conscious.

"I threw her out," he informed her. "And you'll never have to worry about my dallying with another lass, Etta. You don't know me well enough, yet, but I'm loyal to the bone."

Her cheeks tinged with pink, Etta nodded, but still hovered at a distance. "It's not that I don't trust you, Geordie, it's only—it's only that she seems a bit sly, to me."

You don't know the half of it, he thought. With a casual gesture, he indicated the joint stool, near the hearth. "Will you stay and visit for a minute? We may as well get used to each other; I've a few scars, here and there, so don't let it put you off."

Willingly, she dragged the stool over to carefully seat herself beside him, and then was silent for a few moments, as she fingered the towel in her lap. Geordie decided it was a good sign that she couldn't seem to keep her gaze from his chest, again, and remarked in a casual tone, "This was a day, wasn't it?"

The dimple appeared. "Indeed, it was. I am sorry I couldn't tell you more, Geordie; Marcello didn't think it was wise."

"No," Geordie agreed. "And the poor man had enough on his plate, trying to control the gypsies, and answer to the spymaster—all whilst his sister is having her head turned by a rough Scotsman."

"Not so very rough," she protested. "You've been a perfect gentleman."

"I'm restraining myself," he admitted. "You're like a pretty little bluebell, when mainly I've dealt in thistles—although you were a right thistle today, when you rode up, bold as brass, and started jawboning at the Comandante." He chuckled at the memory. "And here I always thought you were mild as milk, lass—it was all I could do not to fall over in surprise."

"I can be mild as milk," she insisted with a smile. "It all depends on the circumstances."

"You're to be your honest self with me, Etta—I wouldn't ask for any less."

With increasing confidence, she rested her hand on his, on the edge of the tub. "I am not familiar with a 'bluebell'. You must show me."

"I will, once we get to Scotland," he promised. "And in turn, you have to show me a bluegill fish, from wherever it is that you hail from."

"Malta," she replied. "We come from the Island of Malta, but I have not been home in a long time."

"That's right—Malta," he repeated, thinking this over. "You lot belong to some sort of church order."

"Yes—the Knights of Malta," she explained. "We go where we are needed."

Rather than delve into her mysterious work, Geordie decided to keep the conversation on lighter topics, since he felt he was making good progress, putting her at ease with him. "Where have you been, that you haven't been home?"

"Algiers, for a time. And then India, and now Spain."

Geordie whistled softly. "You're the one who's well-traveled, lass; small wonder you were teasing me about it."

"I wasn't teasing you—I thought you were wonderful," she replied with all sincerity. "I could have talked with you all day."

"I felt the same, lass—even though I'd the strong sense I was being bamboozled."

"You are very clever," she noted with a smile; "even though you pretend not to be."

He tilted his head. "Rather like you, lass."

The dimple made its appearance again. "Perhaps we are not 'chalk and cheese', after all."

Geordie decided this sentiment deserved a kiss—the lass didn't seem repulsed by his collection of scars, after all—and so he leaned forward to place a gentle hand on the nape of her neck, and draw her toward him. He kissed her softly—still being careful, he was—and duly noted that she didn't seem overly put-off by the gesture, but indeed, seemed a bit eager for more of the same.

With his head close to hers, he murmured, "What a day that was, lass. I was head over heels, and wondering how on heaven's earth I was going to get this Gypsy Queen for myself."

She lifted her face to his, and laughed with delight. "But you managed it. You seem very capable, Geordie."

"Stubborn, instead," he corrected. Still cradling her head, he ran a wet thumb down her cheek. "It was the best assignment I've ever had—although I had to hurry it up a bit, being as you were on your way to your wedding."

She lifted a hand to caress his face in return. "Do you think you can 'hurry it up a bit' now, Geordie?"

"Only hand me the towel," he replied readily.

CHAPTER 41

The following morning, Geordie woke with the dawn, as was his custom, and watched as the light began to filter-in through the window that faced the bed. Etta lay next to him, still sleeping, and he had to smile with the strangeness of it—waking up next to a wife, in a bed, in a house. His life had changed overnight, it seemed, and nothing would ever be the same again. No matter; he was ready for a new challenge—he wasn't one to let the grass grow under his feet, after all.

And as if on cue, he heard a familiar voice, speaking to someone just below his window. *Oh-ho,* he thought; *if I were taking another guess, I'd guess that Ines has spoken with him, and he wants to sound me out.*

Carefully, he withdrew his arm from Etta—fast asleep, the lass was, and it was no surprise; they'd had a busy night. Quietly, he grabbed his clothes and made his way downstairs to the kitchen.

The cook was just stoking-up the fire when Geordie came into the room, unsurprised to behold Minos in quiet conversation with the Padre, as they awaited their breakfast.

"Ho," Geordie said to the Romany man. "Come along, Minos; we're going fishing, again."

Minos raised his head in surprise. "We are, *gadjo*?"

"We are. Let's go."

Geordie grabbed the two poles that stood at the ready near the kitchen door, and then walked down to the river, with Minos hurrying beside him. Geordie asked, "Where's the best place for decent fishing, around here?"

Minos didn't miss a beat, despite the fact that—for all intents and purposes—he shouldn't be familiar with this area. "There is a *charka* over toward those trees." The Romany man gestured to their right. "The fish are very stupid, there." He paused, and then added almost apologetically, "We may wish to stay out of sight, *gadjo*."

Geordie cocked his head, as he directed his steps over toward the copse of trees the other man had indicated. "I'll rely on you, friend, to keep us out of trouble—there's none better, I suspect."

Minos stayed silent, and Geordie smiled to himself, as they came to the quiet area where a portion of the river pooled—a perfect place for fish to bask in the sun.

They set up on the bank, the early morning birds calling overhead just as the morning sun began to filter through the trees. After fishing for a few minutes in silence, Geordie offered, "I suppose the Romanies will be blamed for the Alcazar's destruction. An act of revenge, by the bridegroom's family."

The other man shrugged, as he contemplated his line

in the water. "Everyone always blames the gypsies, *gadjo*. It is nothing new."

Geordie nodded. "It's not all's well that ends well, though; I understand the British spymaster was expecting more from that treasure-casket, and that he's sore disappointed about what was within."

"I hear the same," the smaller man replied. "A terrible shame."

Philosophically, Geordie tilted his head. "Be that as it may, he should be plenty happy with the outcome. Napoleon's base in Spain has been destroyed, and the counterfeiter was extracted—all without the spymaster's having to show his hand."

"We all must take what victories we may," his companion agreed in a pious tone.

Geordie nodded, and casually flicked his line toward a likely shadow. "Will you return to Andalusia, now?"

"I will, *señor*."

"I hear it's beautiful country, up in the mountains."

Minos nodded readily. "*Si*. And there is good fishing, along the Guadalmena River."

Squinting up at the sun, Geordie noted, "Andalusia is where the Spanish *guerrillas* originated, if I remember right. During the war, the *guerrillas* had some legendary leader—El, El—"

"*El Halcon*," Minos supplied. "A very handsome fellow."

"Handsome is as handsome does," Geordie remarked in a dry tone. "I'd say he's more wily than handsome."

"Many would agree," the man replied, unruffled, as he flicked his line outward again.

Geordie smiled slightly, as he contemplated his line. "I'll stand bluff, if that's what you're worried about. I'm a simple soldier, friend, and I figure wiser heads than mine can decide what rightly belongs to who."

"But you are *Ingles, señor*," his companion pointed out, almost apologetically.

"*Escocés*," corrected Geordie, yet again. "There's a big difference, and that's exactly why you can rest easy. The Scots have no more love for the English than you do."

"I have much love for the English," Minos protested. "But the English have much love for the treasure of others."

"I canno' argue with that, friend."

Just then, Geordie felt a strike on his line and walked along the shoreline, patiently winding-in his reel until he could grasp the flopping fish from the water, and efficiently string it along a line. As he crouched, he paused for a moment, because he could hear a horse approaching. On high alert, he turned toward Minos to whistle a warning, but saw—with some surprise—that the other man had vanished.

"Easy," a voice called out. "Pray do not shoot me, Captain."

Geordie straightened up to behold the British spymaster, who casually reined in his horse, so that he stood at a small distance. The two men regarded each other in silence, until the spymaster offered, "You are very unpredictable."

Geordie squinted up at him. "Now, that's where you're wrong, sir, with all due respect. And how was I to know that the Padre was right where he was supposed to be? A bit more debriefing would have been appreciated."

"My apologies," the man offered, bowing his head in acknowledgment. "It was a delicate balance, to keep this group aligned for my purposes, and—given their nature—I was reluctant to reveal too much to anyone."

Since the spymaster hadn't been dealing with a band of gypsies as much as he'd been dealing with a band of seasoned *guerrillas*, Geordie made no comment, and instead reflected on the surprising fact that someone had managed to pull one over on the spymaster—no easy feat, surely. And small wonder, that Geordie had entertained the strong sense that everyone was only humoring him, if the only true Romanies were Gaston and Gerard.

"All's well that ends well," Geordie offered. "What will happen to the Frenchman?"

The spymaster shrugged, slightly. "It is peace time, and so nothing will happen to him."

"That's a right shame," Geordie pronounced, drawing his brows together. "He's a wrong-'un, for sure."

Unruffled, the spymaster continued, "In fact, to add insult to injury, we were obligated to treat his hurts. The injury to his shoulder required that it be re-set by the Alcazar's surgeon." He lifted his gaze to watch the water for a moment. "Poor man—he had to be dosed with laudanum, to do the deed, and whilst under its effects, he revealed some information about future plans—all unknowing, of course."

Lifting his brows, Geordie whistled softly. "Is that so?" Unbidden, he had a sudden memory of Etta, training her pistol on Rochon with steely determination. "It's lucky he wasn't killed in the attack, then—although I know a lot of folks wouldn't have wept for him."

"An unlooked-for boon," the spymaster agreed. "Hopefully, the information we have gleaned will help shorten the next war."

Geordie nodded, and thought, *Now, if I were a superstitious man—like the Romanies—I'd wonder if that's exactly why I was drawn into this plot to begin with; to spare Rochon's life. I'm not a superstitious man, of course, and so instead I'll mark it down as mercy being its own reward.*

The spymaster broke into his thoughts, when he said bluntly, "I am hoping you will reconsider; I have need of men like you."

With a small smile, Geordie shook his head. "Nay, sir. I'm better off doing something honest and open. In fact, I've a mind to try my hand at minting silver coins."

The spymaster stared at him for a long moment. "Whatever do you mean?"

Geordie shrugged. "I hold the mortgage to Colonel Merryfield's silver mines, in Sheffield."

The other's eyes narrowed. "Do you indeed? And how did you manage this?"

"I have the document, fair and square. There's no point in challenging it, friend—I would only tie it up in court. Besides, it's past time to start minting the coins again, if Napoleon's soon to be trouble-causing. I understand you've been shorted another source of income, recently."

There was a small silence. "An extraordinary turn of events," the other observed heavily.

Geordie nodded. "First things, first, though; my wife

and I are going to look up Colonel Merryfield's daughter, and make certain that she's taken care of."

A bit sourly, the other replied, "There is no need; she has managed to land on her feet."

Oh-ho; Geordie thought. *It's just as I suspected; that lass is a handful, and the spymaster must have discovered this for himself.* "Nonetheless, it was his wish, and so I'll go see for myself. And if you pass by his grave, friend, I'd ask that you leave this for him." Geordie reached into his coat pocket, and pulled out his tied-up handkerchief, which now contained his tooth, as well as his military service clasp from the Battle of Badajoz. After contemplating the linen satchel for a moment, he stepped over to hand it to the spymaster. "Give him my regards."

As he took the handkerchief, the other replied in a quiet tone, "He may not be worthy of your regard, Captain."

But Geordie only smiled slightly, and shook his head. "Now, that's where you're wrong, sir, with all due respect —although I canno' tell you more than that." Gathering up his fishing equipment, he then touched the brim of his hat in farewell, and strode away.

CHAPTER 42

After an uneventful trip down the river to the port of Lisbon, Geordie stood with Etta on the busy docks, waiting to catch a ship bound for England. Marcello had accompanied them, and Geordie noted he was deep in conversation with the Captain of the *Sophia*—as though the two men knew each other well.

Gaston stood at a distance, negotiating his passage to the coast of Brittany on another ship. From what Geordie had gleaned, the remnants of the Brittany tribe were to join forces with several other northern tribes, so as to strengthen their numbers. It gave them the best chance for survival—the northern tribes had fared better than the southern ones, in surviving this war.

Adao was slated to accompany Gaston, because it was thought best if the boy disappeared from the Peninsula for a time, being as he was wanted for the supposed murder of Gerard.

"We've always an open door for you," Geordie said to the boy, as Etta smiled her agreement. "Although I imagine you'll be busy. Will the northerners accept you as the *Rom Baro*? You're still but a youngster."

Adao shook his head. "Oh no, *gadjo*; it is Gaston, who will be the *Rom Baro*. The *Alkippa* has made this very plain."

In abject surprise, Geordie stared at him. "*Gaston*? Lord alive, laddie; I don't think he much wants to."

With a small shrug, the boy replied, "He has no choice. A *Rom* does not question the *Alkippa*'s choices."

Thinking this over, Geordie offered, "Then you'll be at loose ends, lad, and you've a canny head on your shoulders. I'll need someone to help me out with the silver mining, if you've a mind to try your hand. You should play least-in sight, anyways, and no better place than the wilds of north England, I reckon. Between us, we can send a cut of the profits back to Gaston."

With a wide smile, Adao nodded eagerly. "I will do it. You are very generous, *gadjo*."

"Not at all; it's what the Colonel wanted, fair and square."

Marcello had finished his conversation with the ship's captain, and now approached them. "The time has come; my best wishes for you both."

"Our door is always open," Geordie replied, grasping the other man's forearms affectionately. "We'll send word, once we're settled, and I imagine we'll visit as soon as Etta decides she's sick o' the rain."

Marcello reminded him, "We have yet to speak of Etta's dowry, Captain."

"Nothin' I need to hear," Geordie replied in a breezy

tone. "I own the rights to a few silver mines, here and there."

Both Etta and Marcello stared at him in surprise. Marcello ventured, "Do you?"

Geordie grinned. "Wouldn't know it to look at me, would you? I think that was half the reason I was given them."

In wonder, Marcello observed, "You are very unpredictable, Captain."

Geordie had to laugh aloud. "No, I'm not, actually—and I think that's the other half of the reason I was given them."

Glancing at Etta, he offered, "I'll give Jenny one last walkabout, if you want to say your goodbyes to your brother." *It must be a wrench for him,* he thought; *they've had many an adventure together, between them. And far be it for me to stand in the way, if more adventuring is called for. I'll let the lass know that I'm not one to shirk a good adventure, myself.*

And so, Geordie led Jenny down the busy docks, thinking about this new chapter in his life, and very content to let it unfold before him. He was idly reviewing a vendor's wares, laid out on a mat, when he heard a voice say in surprise, "Black Bess! Is that you?"

Startled, Geordie looked up to see a man, pausing in wonder to stare at Jenny. Tightening his grip on her halter, Geordie warned, "She's my horse, friend."

The man broke his gaze away from the mare, and assured Geordie, "No—I don't seek a quarrel. She threw me off at Badajoz, but it was the luckiest day of my life, so I can't hold a grudge."

Geordie blinked. *"This horse* threw you off?"

Running a fond hand down Jenny's neck, the man smiled. "Hard to believe, isn't it? She's usually so biddable. She threw me off, the minx, and I lay on the ground with a broken leg, and missed the battle." He sobered, remembering. "It was just as well—not many of us managed to survive that first foray. I was taken-in by a peasant family, and nursed back to health. The fellow needed help with his orchards—his son had died in the war—and so here I am today, sailing to France to buy seedlings, so that I can plant more vineyards. I've married his daughter, and we're starting a winery."

He smiled, and when the horse ducked her head, he willingly rubbed her forehead. "Goodbye, Bessie old girl —I'm glad you managed to find your feet." With a friendly nod to Geordie, he then turned to disappear into the crowd.

Geordie watched him go, as the passersby jostled him on either side. With a mighty effort, he pulled himself together, and turned to lead the horse back to the ship. *You're a hardheaded Scot,* he sternly reminded himself. *Don't be daft; you'll be believing in the pixies, next.*

He made his way to the ship's gangplank, where Etta waited with Adao and Gaston. "Are you ready to board, lass?" he asked.

"I am," she replied steadily, and took his hand in hers.

"Good sailing, *gadjo,*" said Gaston, as he hoisted his duffle to his shoulder.

"Stay in contact, we'll need to send you the funding," Geordie instructed. "I have to say I feel a bit badly, taking

Adao from you. Do you have any kin, where you're going?"

The Romany man shrugged. "I will manage."

Geordie shook his hand. "Good luck to you, then. Don't be a stranger."

With a nod, Gaston turned to make his way toward his own ship.

To Geordie's surprise, Jenny immediately stepped to follow after him, and--after only a moment's hesitation— he released her halter, and watched as the glossy black horse walked away, until she was swallowed up by the crowd.

"Goodbye, lass," he said softly.

With some alarm, Etta looked from one to the other. "Does Gaston take your Jenny?"

Firmly, Geordie nodded. "Indeed, he does, and I can't complain; no need to be selfish, and keep all the Gypsy Queens for myself. "

In sympathy, she squeezed his hand. "Are there good horses, in Sheffield?"

"The English do have good horses," he admitted. "It's one of the few things they do better than the Scots."

"We will find you another, then."

He smiled down into those beautiful eyes—brimful of sympathy, instead of laughter—and promptly forgot about the horse. "You're a rare treat, Etta. I hope you'll be able to tolerate England—I hope I will, for that matter."

Stoutly, she declared, "We will manage it, together. I will go where you go."

He leaned to kiss her. "Then I imagine we'll be back here, and sooner rather than later, if there's to be another war brewing. Your brother will need you, and I'll come along, to look after you."

She was silent for a moment, and then her next words were heartfelt. "Thank you, Geordie. I would like that, very much."

He took a long breath. "I suppose you'll bristle at me again, if I ask you not to risk yourself."

With a smile, she glanced up at him, her eyes alight with humor. "I would do it a hundred times more, if you have need of another extraction."

Shaking his head in wonder, he replied, "I knew there was more to you than it seemed. You broke your role for a minute, back in the Senora's dining room, when you told me not to tell you what to do."

"I don't like being told what to do," she admitted.

With a grin, he gazed down at her. "I was that smitten, lass; but I always had the sense you were laughing at me."

"Not at you," she insisted. "I was laughing because I knew I'd met my fate in you, and who would have predicted it?"

Jenny, thought Geordie, as he drew her close, and then scolded himself for being as superstitious as the Romanies.